THE ELEPHANT-HEADED GOD
AND OTHER
HINDU TALES

Rama and the Sea God (see page 4)

THE ELEPHANT-HEADED GOD

AND OTHER
HINDU TALES

RETOLD BY

DEBJANI CHATTERJEE

WITH ILLUSTRATIONS BY
MARGARET JONES

OXFORD UNIVERSITY PRESS
NEW YORK

*With love and hope for my nephews
Anirvan and Nikhilendu and
all the world's children*

Oxford University Press

Oxford   New York   Toronto
Delhi   Bombay   Calcutta   Madras   Karachi
Kuala Lumpur   Singapore   Hong Kong   Tokyo
Nairobi   Dar es Salaam   Cape Town
Melbourne   Auckland   Madrid
and associated companies in
Berlin   Ibadan

Published 1992 by Oxford University Press, Inc.,
200 Madison Avenue, New York, New York 10016

Oxford is a registered trademark of Oxford University Press

Library of Congress Cataloging-in-Publication Data

Chatterjee, Debjani.
The elephant-headed god and other Hindu tales /
Debjani Chatterjee.
p.   cm.
Summary: A collection of Hindu myths featuring gods and goddesses,
kings and queens, heroes and beggars, angelic beings and demons.
ISBN 0-19-508112-9
1. Mythology, Hindu—Juvenile literature.
2. Tales—India—Juvenile literature. [1. Mythology, Hindu.] I. Title.
BL1111.2.c43 1992
294.5'13—dc20   92-20454
CIP
AC

Printing (last digit): 9 8 7 6 5 4 3 2 1

Printed in the United States of America
on acid-free paper

Contents

A list of main characters

Bali The demon-king of Patal (Hell) whom Vishnu subdues.

Bhasmasura A demon who tried to destroy Shiva.

Brahma God the Creator. He is the first god of the Hindu trinity of Brahma, Vishnu and Shiva.

Ganesh Also called Ganesha and Ganapati, the elephant-headed god of Wisdom and the Remover of Obstacles. He is the son of Parvati and Shiva.

Hanuman A monkey chief whose father is the god Vayu and who is Rama's devoted friend.

Himalaya The greatest mountain range in the world, the name means Place of Snow. Also Parvati's father and a god of the mountains.

Indra King of the gods and a rain-giver, he rules over Indraloka (Heaven), but is subject to the great gods: Brahma, Vishnu and Shiva.

Karna Kunti's son by Surya, the Sun-god.

Krishna Philosopher-king of Dwarka and an incarnation of Vishnu. His teachings are found in the *Bhagavad Gita* (Divine Song).

Kunti Pandu's elder wife and mother of the Pandava princes, Yudhishtira, Bhima and Arjuna.

Parvati Her name means Daughter of the Mountain. She is the daughter of Himalaya and is Shiva's wife.

Rama Prince of Ayodhya (present day Oudh or Awadh) and hero of the *Ramayana* epic.

Shibi A king known for his kindness and hospitality.

Shiva He is Destroyer of Evil, god of yoga and Parvati's husband. He rides upon Nandi, his bull.

Vishnu God the Preserver. He incarnates himself to save mankind and to destroy evildoers. Some of his incarnations mentioned in this book are: Rama, Krishna, Parasurama and the Dwarf.

Author's Foreword

These stories come from ancient India, but they belong to children everywhere and in every age. They tell of a fabulous world peopled by gods and goddesses, angelic beings and demons, kings and queens, heroes and beggars. It is a world that is brought to life by your curiosity and imagination.

These stories are among the oldest in the world. They contain voices from hundreds of years ago. When you read them, judge for yourself if those voices have something to say to children of today.

Debjani Chatterjee

The Monkey Bridge to Lanka

LET ME tell you the tale of how, many years ago, the animals helped Rama, prince of Ayodhya, to rescue his beloved wife Sita. It is a tale of courage, of strength and patient endurance; and above all it is a tale of unity, loyalty, and friendship. The monkeys played a most important part, but there were many heroes of the animal world who came at Rama's call and all did their humble best.

By a cruel fate, and even though they had done nothing wrong, Rama and Sita had been banished to the forests of north India for fourteen years. But instead of being downcast they tried to make their lives in the forest as happy as possible. Nor were they lonely, for not only was Rama's younger brother, Lakshman, with them to share their exile, but they soon made friends with the birds and animals of the forest. With their bows and arrows, Rama and Lakshman would defend their new friends against the demons who would come from time to time to attack them. All the animals loved the gentle princess Sita.

One day, Ravana, the ten-headed and twenty armed demon-king, seized Sita when she was walking alone in the forest, and dragged her into his flying chariot. Desperate that her husband would not know where she had gone, Sita took off her colourful bangles, tinkling anklets, earrings, nose-ring and necklace, and threw them one by one from the chariot, in the hope that Rama might find them and follow the trail to rescue her. The jewellery fell into dense jungles as Ravana drove his chariot southward across the sky, heading back to his island kingdom of Lanka.

The forest animals heard Sita's cries as the wicked Ravana bore her away, and they were filled with pity for her. Swinging from branch to branch, the monkeys tried to follow the chariot, but it was too swift for them. They did, however, note where Sita's jewellery fell, so that they could show them to Rama afterwards. The animals were all frightened of Ravana but Jatayu, the great eagle, bravely tried to stop the demon-king by swooping down and attacking him with his sharp beak and talons. After a fierce fight Ravana slashed off Jatayu's wings with his sword and the dying bird fell to the forest floor. With his last breath Jatayu described Sita's kidnapper to Rama and Lakshman, who now realised that their enemy was the mighty Ravana. Rama blessed the noble bird and asked him to close his eyes as he prayed. Then Jatayu saw in a vision that the prince whom he had helped was none other than the great god Vishnu born on Earth to punish the demon-king! The eagle died content.

Determined to rescue Sita, Rama and Lakshman set off on foot through jungles and over mountains, following the trail. The monkeys warned them that Ravana would never give up Sita without a fight and the demon-king was reputed to have a large and terrifying army of demons. They offered to accompany the two princes and serve as their army. Along the way they came across other animals and many of these too, especially the bears and elephants, decided to join Rama in fighting the evil Ravana.

So, accompanied by his brother and by a large army of animals, Rama reached the southern tip of India. There he found the vast Indian Ocean blocking his way! Rama knew that the tear-shaped island of Lanka lay not far across the water, glittering like a jewel in the sun, with its many splendid palaces and fortresses ringed by gardens full of peacocks and deer. Somehow, Rama, who had no flying chariot like the demon-king, had to find a way across the ocean.

Though he was really Vishnu living on Earth as a man, Rama now prayed for help in his difficulty, like any ordinary man. He stood by the ocean shore and prayed to the god of the seas. The sea god was troubled as he sat on his throne in his underwater palace of coral and shells. Every sincere prayer is heard by the gods, and so he could not help hearing Rama. But, he reasoned, the sea is the sea. He could not dry up the ocean just to let Rama and his friends walk across! So he ordered the sea nymphs to come and play music on their conches, hoping that he could drown the sound of Rama's prayers! But it was a vain hope. The prince of Ayodhya prayed the harder, and Lakshman and the monkeys joined him. The sea god grew more and more troubled, but still he did nothing.

At length Rama felt that he could wait no longer. Every hour that passed was an hour apart from his beloved wife who was now in captivity. He was angry, too, because the god of the seas was deliberately ignoring their prayers. It was necessary, he decided, to teach the god a lesson. Now Rama was the best archer in all of India. With his eyes kindling with anger, he pulled out a special arrow from his quiver. Aiming carefully he let it fly into the ocean. The arrow sped through the water until it found its target. The barbed point bit painfully into one shoulder of the sea god. The god of the seas knew that he had angered a hero far greater than himself. With the white froth, flecked with his blood, bubbling around him, he rose to the surface. Very humbly he joined his hands as he faced the prince who was about to loose a second arrow.

"Please don't shoot, great Rama! I beg your forgiveness for my mistake," said the trembling god. "I am only a minor god of the seas, while you are almighty Vishnu and the whole of creation is in your keeping. I know that your heart is full of sorrow for Sita who is a prisoner in Lanka. But I cannot dry up the ocean for your army to walk across, for many living creatures would suffer and die if I did. What would happen to the fish that swim and play in the sea? And what of the sailors who sail on it, and the fishermen who fish in its waters?"

Rama sighed and put away his bow. He knew what the sea god said was true and his words melted away his anger. "I am going mad thinking of how Sita must be suffering. There must be some way that you can help me," he urged.

The sea nymphs and dolphins who had risen to the surface of the ocean in support of their king, looked imploringly at the sea god, as did the monkeys on the shore.

The god was thoughtful as he pulled out Rama's arrow. He rubbed his shoulder, and the wound healed instantly. "I have it!" he said suddenly, a bright smile lighting up an already radiant face. "I will give what help I can, but you will all have to help yourselves first. Throw sticks, stones, anything, into the water. I will support every grain of sand and splinter of wood you throw in, so that it floats on the ocean, until a floating bridge to Lanka is formed." Having given his promise of help, the sea god and his companions disappeared in the swirling waters.

"But it will take an age to build," protested Lakshman.

"Let's start right away then!" suggested Rama.

The two brothers and the animals got busy. Great apes and huge bears hurled massive boulders into the sea. Elephants uprooted giant trees with their trunks and carried them to the water. Even the birds carried twigs in their beaks. Monkeys of all sizes and colours competed to see who could carry the most stones.

After some hours of frantic effort, one of the monkeys stopped for a rest. His attention was caught by a little brown squirrel that was busily scurrying between the sea and the sand. The squirrel was energetically rolling on the beach to collect sand and dust in its soft fur, then it was rushing to the water and shaking the sand and dust off its bushy tail and body. The macaque roared with laughter, and all the other monkeys came running to see what the fun was, for they are easily distracted. They all laughed too when they saw the little squirrel trying to help build the bridge with its puny efforts. It seemed quite ridiculous to them. One of the monkeys went across to tell Rama that while he was throwing boulders and trees in the water, a foolish squirrel was shaking dust into it.

"Why! It might as well not bother!" he jeered.

At once the prince went to where quite a crowd had collected. He, too, saw the squirrel rolling on the sand while the monkeys laughed. But Rama only smiled and very gently he picked up the squirrel and placed it on the palm of one hand.

"Friend," said Rama, and his voice was full of love, "all here are helping me to build a bridge to Lanka. The monkeys of course are doing a tremendous job. In generations to come, children will hear of the mighty Monkey Bridge to Lanka. Poets will sing the praises of the apes and the chimpanzees. But every creature that helps me is my friend. Everyone here has my undying gratitude. You, little one, are working as hard as anyone. I am truly grateful for your help."

While the other animals looked on in wonder and a little shame, Rama blessed the squirrel. With his free hand he gently stroked its back, saying: "You shall carry forever a mark of my love and gratitude."

To the astonishment of those gathered around, Rama's fingers left five stripes on the squirrel's back. How proud it was! Now the squirrel's part in building the bridge would never be forgotten.

Ravana, the demon-king, had laughed in contempt when his spies had brought him reports that Rama had amassed a monkey army in the forests of south India. He had laughed too when they reported that the army had reached the ocean shore. When he heard that they were busy building a bridge to cross over to Lanka, he laughed so much that everyone thought he would burst.

"They are mad," thundered the scornful tyrant. "No one can build a bridge over the ocean. They will die of old age long before they succeed!"

It did not take long, however, for Ravana's spies to discover that rocks and stones were floating magically on the water, and before their unbelieving eyes a bridge was taking shape. Ravana did not believe them when they reported this latest news. Calling them "fools and dunderheads", he ordered them to be hung upside down while their toes were tickled with feathers. But later that day as he walked upon the terrace of his favourite palace, Ravana saw, to his horror, a bridge that truly stretched out from India towards Lanka.

For a moment the demon-king grew pale with fear. But he still refused to return Sita to her husband, choosing instead to face Rama in battle. The story of that great battle, where good was ranged against evil, Rama against Ravana, the monkeys against the demons, is a favourite tale that is often told. The outcome, as you may expect, was that Ravana was killed and his hordes of demons defeated. The victorious Rama and Lakshman rescued Sita and crowned Ravana's good younger brother as the new king, to the general delight of the people of Lanka. Then they flew back with Sita to their own kingdom of Ayodhya in Ravana's flying chariot. In Ayodhya there was great rejoicing to see them alive and safe. Every home was decorated and lamps were lit in their honour. Rama and Lakshman's old father had died in their absence, so Rama now became king, and Sita his queen. Rama's reign is still talked about in India as a "golden age", for it was a time of great happiness for all good people.

The Monkey Bridge to Lanka has long since collapsed into the sea. But even today, thousands of years later, Hindus all over the world decorate their homes each year during Diwali, the Festival of Lights, to celebrate the triumphant return of Rama and Sita. To this day, squirrels all over India carry the mark of Rama's gratitude; and when the tide is low the water is quite shallow in places between India and the tear-shaped island of Sri Lanka. On quiet nights, fisherfolk hear the sea nymphs sing of the famous Monkey Bridge, and one is almost tempted to walk across.

The Elephant-Headed God

J UST look at the picture opposite this page. Take a
good long look. You cannot help smiling, can you?
Look at that elephant head sitting quite casually,
and absurdly, on a fat boy's neck - he's so fat in fact that
I think his neck's disappeared! Have you ever heard of a
boy with an elephant's head? You will notice too that one
of the tusks is broken. Can you see it? If you look
carefully, you may spy a small rat in the picture too.

This strange creature is Ganesh, the popular elephant-
headed god. I don't think that he minds you smiling or
even laughing at him - most people do the first time that
they see him - for he is a jolly and friendly god with a great
sense of humour. That elephant's head on his shoulders is
no joke, however.

You may have heard that the Hindus worship many
gods and goddesses who are all different aspects of the
one God. Ganesh is an important god in many ways. He
is very near and dear to mankind, whom he is always
helping. He is "the Remover of Obstacles" - so when
Hindus have problems or difficulties, big or small, they
turn to him. He brings good luck to his worshippers, and
many Indian merchants and shopkeepers keep pictures or
little carved images of him in the home, the office or even
the car! But Ganesh is, above all, the god of Wisdom.

Wisdom? Well, why not? That elephant head has
something to do with it. He only became the god of
Wisdom, you see, after he acquired the elephant head.
Hindus have always loved their elephants for their hard

work, loyalty and gentleness. But they also respect the elephant for its great wisdom, long memory and dignity. With its wisdom and its strength the elephant is more truly the king of the animal world than any lion can be.

To learn the secret of how Ganesh got his elephant's head, I must tell you something about his parents. I am sure you will agree that it is the strangest tale of all!

Ganesh belongs to the most popular family of gods in Hinduism. He is the elder son of Parvati and Shiva. Parvati is the daughter of the Himalayas, that snowy chain of mountains that covers the north of India. She is a most beautiful and gracious goddess, a loving mother and devoted wife. Shiva - well, even his best friends will admit that he is not exactly an ideal father or husband. Shiva loves his family dearly, in his own way. It's just that he cannot bear to stay at home all the time. He has a wanderlust in him and likes to go travelling on his pet bull. Unfortunately, the places he is really keen on are remote and dangerous mountains and icy peaks - not the sort of places one takes one's family for a picnic!

Shiva likes the peace of cremation grounds too. But his great passion is yoga-meditation. He cannot get enough of it and, when absorbed in meditation, even an earthquake does not disturb him. Shiva has other strange habits too. He dislikes wearing a lot of clothes, and is happiest wandering about barefoot with only a tiger skin around his waist. Naturally many gods think that he is quite mad, and everyone thought that Parvati too must have lost her senses when she married him.

For some time after his marriage Shiva was supremely happy, living with Parvati in a little cottage on Mount Kailas in the Himalayas, far away from human civilisation and far also from Indra's glittering court in heaven and all other disturbances. But after a while Parvati could see that her husband was getting restless. He would open the window and look longingly at the high mountain peaks, and a dreamy look would come into his eyes. Because she loved him deeply, Parvati understood his innermost wishes.

One day she said to Shiva, "Why don't you go away for a while? I know that you led a different life before we married. You used to meditate, and sometimes danced on cremation grounds along with your ghosts and banshee friends. You must be missing all that now."

"No, dear one," assured her husband. "My wild days are over. I really don't need them now."

"But don't you miss your companions?" she persisted.

"When I look at you, I don't notice their absence!" Shiva smiled at her mischievously. "The truth is that the ghosts, demons and banshees are all around the house, for they are never far from me. I did not wish to frighten you, so I ordered them to be invisible and to keep very quiet; and how well they have obeyed me!"

Parvati was torn between alarm and laughter - alarm at the thought of being surrounded by creatures from a nightmare world, and laughter at Shiva's absurd pride in his friends. Shiva pleaded, "You won't ask me to send them away, will you? They are like little children - naughty at times, but they mean no harm. Why, they all love you already, for they know that you are my wife. And I know that you could not be cruel to anyone."

Parvati agreed that Shiva's companions could stay.

"What about your meditation, then?" she asked. "That used to be your main occupation. You are the greatest yogi among the gods. But even you must keep in practice. And your bull, Nandi, hasn't had any exercise for ages!"

Shiva knew that she was right. He longed to be absorbed once more in the joy of meditation, and he truly missed all his favourite mountain spots where he sat and meditated. It was, after all, his mastery of yoga that had made him a god of such great power. But still he hesitated.

"Will you not be lonely if I go?" he asked. "There is no one here but the demons, and they will follow me if I go."

Parvati assured him that she would be perfectly happy on her own. She wanted to transform their cottage, which was really no more than a bare hovel, into a comfortable and lovely place to raise a family - a real home.

So a happy Shiva stripped to his tiger skin, wrapped his favourite snakes about him, and shouted to Nandi who came galloping to his master. Waving goodbye, Shiva set off on his bull, with his wierd assortment of friends.

"I won't be long," he told Parvati.

Parvati, appealing to all the ghosts, said, "Guard my husband well!"

But Shiva is a most forgetful god. And when he is meditating it is virtually impossible to rouse him. High above the sacred river Ganges, at Gangotri, Shiva sat and meditated. Many years passed, which were thousands of human years - for time is different for gods and men. When at last Shiva rose from his lotus pose, he remembered his wife waiting patiently at home on Mount Kailas, and hurriedly made his way back to her.

In the meantime Parvati had planted a lovely garden around the cottage, sewn curtains for the windows, cushions for the floor, and painted the doors and walls. She was not alone for very long, either. Shiva did not know that he had left his wife pregnant. In time Parvati had a handsome baby boy who kept her very busy indeed. She named him Ganesh. The years passed and the baby god grew into a

quiet thoughtful little boy who was very attached to his mother and loved to help her in any way. He often asked Parvati about his father, and she told him that Shiva was one of the very greatest of the gods, far greater than Indra who was the king of heaven.

One spring morning Parvati was enjoying a bath, while her son stood by the garden gate. A tall stranger with long matted hair, snakes wriggling about him, and wearing only an animal skin, strode up to the gate. Nandi, the bull, followed behind, for the stranger was of course none other than Shiva. He had rushed home without bothering to tidy up his wild appearance.

Shiva hesitated as he looked at the sun-bathed cottage with flowering creepers and bushes and sweet smelling herbs around it. Was this beautiful home really his? And who was the handsome boy who blocked his way?

"Let me pass, boy," said Shiva gruffly, for he was impatient to see his dear wife again.

"No," said Ganesh, frowning at the dirty vagabond trying to force his way in. "You may not enter."

But brushing the boy aside, Shiva walked straight through the garden to the house. Ganesh knew that his mother was bathing inside the cottage, and that this rude fellow must be prevented at all cost from entering. He rushed to the door and drew out his sword. Poor boy! What a moment to rouse his father's anger. Shiva is a most quick-tempered god, though he is quick to forgive as well. Now he lost his temper completely. Shiva's third eye of power blazed fire from the middle of his forehead, and in seconds a headless and helpless body was all that lay between him and the cottage door.

On hearing voices, Parvati had quickly stepped out of the bath. She opened the door, only to find her son without a head and her long absent husband eager to embrace her. She tore herself from his arms and wept bitterly. Nandi, the bull, whimpered in sympathy.

"What have you done? What have you done?" she repeated, wringing her hands. "That is our son whom you have destroyed!" Her grief was dreadful to see.

Shiva was truly sorry now. He tried to comfort her. "Our son is a god, so he is not dead. He is only stunned for a while. I haven't destroyed him, only his head. He does not really need a head to be himself."

But Parvati would have none of it. "You have destroyed him, crazy yogi that you are! What use is a god without a head?"

Shiva tried his best to convince her that no great harm had been done. After all, he had once destroyed the entire body of Kama, the god of Love. And everyone knows what an active god Kama is. He does not need a body to roam through the universe, shooting his arrows. But Parvati insisted that Shiva restore Ganesh's head.

"But I can't undo what I've already done!" Shiva protested.

It was no use. He felt desperate. He simply could not bear to listen to Parvati weeping.

At length Shiva promised to bring back the head of the first sleeper he met who was lying in the "wrong position". Hindus believe that it is best to sleep along the earth's magnetic line, with the head towards the North Pole and the feet pointing towards the South Pole. Someone sleeping in the "wrong position" would, therefore, do just the opposite, and have his or her head towards the south and feet towards the north.

After searching for several miles, Shiva came across a baby elephant that was sleeping in the wrong position.

Shiva had already given his word. He had not said that he would bring back the first boy's head, or even a human head, so now it was the baby elephant's head he removed. Shiva quickly returned to the cottage with the elephant head and placed it on his son's shoulders.

A baby's head is very big and heavy, especially when it is that of a baby elephant. So Ganesh found it difficult to balance his new head at first, with its long wriggly trunk and large fan-like ears. Parvati was horrified to see Ganesh's new head. Shiva really must be mad, she thought. Her poor son! He would surely become the laughing stock of heaven! She decided to ask help of the other gods and goddesses, on behalf of Ganesh.

Parvati lifted her son in her arms and flew up with him, straight to heaven. She did not stop till she found herself in Indra's court. A hush came over all the gods and goddesses when they saw a weeping Parvati carrying a strange little boy with an elephant head. Indra and his queen rose from their golden thrones to greet Parvati.

"Gracious goddess," said the king of heaven, "we have sadly missed you since your marriage. And now you come to us with tears in your beautiful eyes. You have only to command us. In what way may we help you?" Other gods and goddesses too came crowding around Parvati, for she is much loved in heaven and on earth.

Parvati told them about Ganesh's accident and begged Indra to give Ganesh a proper head instead.

"I do understand how you feel, Parvati," said Indra. "But what you suggest is impossible. I am king of all the lesser gods and goddesses. But Shiva and you are far greater than I. There is nothing that I can do which is not in your power to do as well. If Shiva has given your son an elephant head, it must be what is best for the boy."

Shachi, the queen of heaven, had a suggestion. It was true that no god or goddess was greater than Shiva, and Parvati who was his equal was too unhappy to think calmly about what was best for Ganesh, but Shachi reminded them that there were two other gods who were also Shiva's equals in power. They were Brahma the Creator, and Vishnu the Preserver. Hindus believe that Brahma, Vishnu and Shiva are three equal aspects of God.

No sooner did Shachi mention their names than the two great gods appeared.

"My brother gods, have pity on my innocent son," pleaded Parvati. "Must he suffer like this for his father's quick temper and madness?"

Both the gods asked Parvati to dry her tears, for all would be well. Brahma, who loves children, sat on Indra's throne and seated Ganesh on his knee. Vishnu smiled at Parvati and asked her to forgive her husband. "Shiva did not know what he was doing when his third eye burnt away Ganesh's head. But your son has lost nothing by it. He is lucky to be the son of Shiva and Parvati, and he will become a great god in his own right. He may not be a handsome god any more, but all will recognise his goodness and love him for himself. Alone among the gods and goddesses, he has an elephant head, so he will never be forgotten or ignored and will have a special place in heaven and in the hearts of people."

Actually, Brahma thought the elephant head was rather attractive. Both Brahma and Vishnu showered their blessings on the boy and gave him special gifts.

"Ganesh with his elephant head will be the god of Wisdom," said Brahma. "Writers will worship him. He will be the scribe of heaven, and the god of Literature."

"He will be the Remover of Obstacles," added Vishnu,

"and will be worshipped first at any religious ceremony, before any other gods are worshipped. He is the god who will smile good fortune on any new undertaking."

Parvati felt much happier now, even though Ganesh still had an elephant head. She warmly thanked all the gods and goddesses.

Shiva was waiting at the cottage on Mount Kailas. He knew what was happening at Indra's court, for he could see it all with his magical third eye. When Parvati returned with their son, Shiva lovingly welcomed them.

To this day, Ganesh lives happily with his parents. He also lives in the hearts of his worshippers. He is now a plump god who can easily support his elephant head. All religious festivals for Hindus begin with his worship and many books by Hindus have, at the beginning, a prayer to the elephant-headed god of Wisdom.

Brahma and Vishnu were right. The elephant-headed god is much loved by Hindus. Hindus also love to tell, and listen to, the many stories about Ganesh's kindness and friendliness, his love of food, and his wisdom.

As well as being the god of Wisdom, Ganesh was also made the scribe of heaven. When Indra, the king of heaven, has any important proclamation to be written down, when some god wants a letter written to a shy goddess, or when the twin gods of Medicine have a lengthy prescription to write, they all ask Ganesh to help, for he has most beautiful handwriting, is exceptionally good at spelling, and can write astonishingly fast - almost at the speed of thought! Oh, one other thing. I did not mention the fact that his is no ordinary pen. In his chubby right hand, Ganesh holds part of an ivory elephant tusk which he dips in ink and writes with! There is an interesting story behind this.

It happened in this way. Thousands of years ago, the wise sage Vyasa wanted to compose a long and beautiful poem to tell the history of his people and teach them to live noble lives. But it would be such a long poem that Vyasa feared he might not live to finish writing it, for he was an old man. In his difficulty, Vyasa prayed to Ganesh.

"You are the scribe of the gods, Ganesh," the old man prayed, "but will you work for me, for a change? If you do not write down at my dictation my work will be lost to the world. But I am poor and have nothing to pay you with. Indeed, what can one offer a god for such a service? You must work for the joy of listening to my words alone."

You might think that Ganesh would have had enough on his hands without coming and slaving away for weeks and perhaps months for an old man whose poem would probably turn out to be dreadfully boring anyway, especially if it was going to be full of history and teachings. But Ganesh is a most generous god. He was sorry for the old sage and wanted to help him, even though he had his doubts about how good his poem might be.

The god agreed to help Vyasa on one condition.

"Once you start dictating you must not stop till you come to the end. I will write down your words as fast as you recite them. But if at any time you pause for thought or rest, I shall get bored and stop writing immediately. I'm afraid your work will then remain incomplete."

The old man was overjoyed to have the god of Wisdom working as his scribe. Afraid to delay even for a moment in case Ganesh got bored before he started, or changed his mind, Vyasa hurriedly started reciting his poem. A little taken aback at such speed, Ganesh glanced about him for something to write with. He had not come prepared with a pen. But the words of the old poet were ringing in his elephant head, and they were of marvellous power and beauty. Anxious not to lose a single word from the wise Vyasa's lips, and completely forgetting everything except for his need to write down the poem, Ganesh broke off half of his left tusk and dipped it in ink.

The result of this extraordinary partnership of man and god is the longest poem in the world - it has about 180,000 lines - and one of the best. It is called the *Mahabharata*, which means "The Great Story of India". You may like to read it yourself one day.

Do you remember the rat mentioned at the beginning of this story of the elephant-headed god, the rat who is always in pictures of Ganesh? He was once a proud and wicked monster. Frightened people prayed to Ganesh to save them from this terrible giant. When Ganesh told the monster to stop bullying people, he simply laughed, for he did not believe that Ganesh could stop him. So the god lifted one foot, and squashing the giant to the ground, turned him into a lowly rat. But Ganesh is so kindhearted that he would not abandon the monster after he had become a little rat. Besides, the monster was now sorry that he had been so wicked and promised to turn over a new leaf. Ganesh, therefore, decided to keep the rat near him always as his pet.

The Hindu gods and goddesses have special animals to ride upon. Shiva's pet, of course, is Nandi the bull. Indra rides upon a white elephant. The goddess Durga rides a tiger. So the rat became Ganesh's pet; and you may not believe it, but Ganesh rides upon the rat whenever he has to go anywhere! You see, for a god - especially such an unusual god as Ganesh - all things are possible.

The Race

THIS is a story about Ganesh's wisdom, his devotion to his mother, and the rivalry between him and his younger brother.

No two brothers could be more different. Kartikeya, the younger son of Shiva and Parvati, is a most handsome god - and he knows it! Tall, slim and athletic, Kartikeya is god of War and is accomplished in using all weapons. Like some young boys he is also rather vain about his appearance and abilities. Appropriately, his symbol and pet is the peacock, the most beautiful of all birds and the national bird of India. Kartikeya enjoyed energetic games and contests where he could compete with other gods, especially with his elder brother, and of course win.

One day Kartikeya was teasing his plump elder brother and challenged him to a race! Ganesh was used to his ways, so he smiled but continued reading a book.

"Look mother," Kartikeya appealed, "he does nothing but poke his trunk in a book all day long. Tell him that we gods should fly around and patrol the world once in a while. I'm flying about all the time on my peacock. I am surely a better god than he is?"

"We shall see," was Parvati's answer. Then she set her sons a little test. She asked them both to go once around the universe and whoever returned first would be the winner. Parvati would give the winner a special blessing.

Kartikeya leapt up in excitement. "I'll get on my peacock right away and I'll be back in no time at all," he boasted. The young god laughed to think of Ganesh riding on his tiny rat. It would take him millions, maybe billions or even zillions of years to go around the universe. "You may as well give up right now," said Kartikeya, "because you haven't a hope of winning!"

Waving a cheery goodbye, Kartikeya was off on his colourful bird. Ganesh just sat and quietly thought for a moment. He joined the palms of his hands together and bowed his head in prayer to the Goddess Parvati. Then he climbed on his rat and very slowly, full of dignity, he began to ride in a circle around his mother.

It took Kartikeya a full day and a night to fly once around the entire universe. So swiftly did he fly that he hardly saw the planets, stars and moons, that went whizzing past. At last, happy and proud, Kartikeya presented himself to his mother, fully expecting to be greeted as the winner.

But, "Kartikeya, it is your brother who was first," were Parvati's astonishing words. The goddess knew that her younger son needed to be taught a lesson if he was to grow up. "Your speed was no match for his wisdom!"

Kartikeya could hardly believe that he had heard correctly. But he knew that his mother always spoke the truth. He turned to Ganesh and asked curiously, "How did you manage it? How can you go around the universe so quickly on your rat?"

"Little brother, our mother who gave us birth and who looks after us, is also the Creator of everything and everyone in the universe. The sun rises in the east, the stars shine at night, the birds sing, the rivers flow, only because our mother wills it. When you see people, animals, trees, mountains, even gods, you are reminded of the great Mother who made all. We are all part of her. She *is* the universe! So I simply went around her," explained Ganesh.

Kartikeya at once understood what his brother was trying to say and felt ashamed of his earlier pride and boasting. He humbly asked Ganesh to pardon him and then bowed to Parvati.

"Mother, will you also forgive me? Because you are so loving and I am young and foolish, I think of you as mine only. I forget that you are the universal Mother."

Parvati stretched out her graceful arms and tenderly called both gods to her.

"My sons, you are both winners," she said. "A mother's love is freely given and there can be no child who fails to win her blessing. You both have my blessings. May you, in turn, be a blessing to all who call to you in their need."

Shiva and the Mountain

AFTER their marriage, Shiva and Parvati lived simply and very happily on Shiva's mountain home of Kailas. But Parvati's father, Himalaya, pitied his daughter when he and his wife, Mena, visited them one day.

"How poorly they live!" he said to Mena. "My lovely child wears no jewellery. Her servants are ghosts and goblins! Shiva has given her caves and mud huts when she deserves palaces! Alas! Why did my daughter marry this naked beggar whose clothes are snakes and ashes?"

"For Parvati's sake we must put on a cheerful face," said Mena. "After all, she claims to be supremely happy."

They did not stay long, for newly-weds should be left alone together as much as possible; but after several years had passed, they began to miss their daughter very much.

"She is not even living near us any more," complained the mountain lord. "That crazy fellow has taken her to Varanasi, his city on sinful Earth. It must be awful! All the dead and the dying are brought to Varanasi. It will be one vast cremation ground for Shiva to dance on! And our sweet daughter is caught up in all this!"

"Enough!" said Mena. "Why don't you go to Shiva's city and see our daughter?"

So it was that Himalaya, taking his human form, set off on the long journey to see his daughter and son-in-law. He was very proud of the fact that he was lord of the highest mountain range in the world! From his treasure store, he selected his choicest jewels and gathered many fine clothes to take to his daughter whose husband could give her nothing.

On his way, Himalaya came across a beggar with long matted hair. "Tell me, fellow, am I on the right road for Varanasi?" asked the lord of mountain ranges.

To his surprise, the beggar answered, "Yes, this is the way to Shiva's city which opens the door to heaven. But you must improve your manners if you hope to enter! Shiva's terrible demon, Kala Bhairav, guards the city and only those who come in humility may enter."

"Nonsense!" said Himalaya, "I am lord of the highest and mightiest of mountains. My wealth and power will gain me entry into even the greatest of kingdoms."

Now the beggar was really Shiva in disguise, but his father-in-law did not recognise him. "Beware!" he cautioned, "You are mighty only by God's grace. I will tell you the story of my friend, the sage Agastya. The Vindhya mountains were proud and reaching towards heaven! God sent Agastya from Varanasi to bring down the mountain. When he crossed the Vindhyas, the mountain range bowed to the holy man in respect. 'I am visiting south India,' said Agastya. 'Do not rise up till I return.' But he never returned. He settled down in the south and the Vindhyas remain bowed low to this day. Otherwise you could not boast of being lord of the mightiest mountains."

Himalaya felt somewhat humbled now. He thanked the beggar for his wise words and continued on his way.

After a while he saw the horizon lit up. As he came nearer, he rubbed his eyes in wonder. Across the Varana River was a magnificent sight - the glittering city of Varanasi! It was a city of palaces whose tall towers seemed endless in their height. The streets were strewn with gold while precious stones of many colours sparkled

in the buildings. It was a city of gardens too, where every tree bore marvellous fruits and seemed like the magical Parijata tree of Indraloka, whose leaves perfume the heavens. Coiled like a silver necklace around the city lay Heaven's own river, the goddess Ganga!

"Can this be Varanasi?" thought the amazed traveller. "Is this the city ruled by my vagabond son-in-law?"

Suddenly an immense black demonic figure blocked his path. Kala Bhairav!

"Who are you and why have you come to Shiva's city?" thundered the giant.

Himalaya might have answered that he was the mighty lord of all mountains, or even that he was the father-in-law of Varanasi's ruler. But a change had come over him.

Instead he replied,"This is the city where all souls find their freedom when they meet god. I too have come to meet him. Shiva is lord of all creation and his wealth cannot be measured. All that I have, I have by his grace. So I have come to thank him and to worship him."

"Enter," said Kala Bhairav, making way for him.

Himalaya forgot that he had brought rich gifts for his daughter. Instead he used his wealth to build yet another temple in honour of Shiva, and there the great Himalaya, worshipped the god.

Parvati and Shiva at once appeared to him. "This temple shall be called Shaileshvara, the Mountain's God," said Shiva most graciously. "All who worship here will find freedom for their souls, just as you have done."

India's holy city has known many invasions and seen the destruction of countless of its old temples. But Himalaya's temple, Shaileshvara, still stands. You will need to journey yourself to Varanasi some day, if you wish to test the truth of Shiva's promise to his father-in-law!

Ashes to Ashes

AS LORD of all demons, Shiva has some extremely strange followers, and occasionally they are even a danger to him! But even though the great god has a tender heart for those creatures who are normally rejected by society, this compassion sometimes leads him into trouble.

Once there was a demon called Bhasmasura who decided to ask Lord Shiva's help so that he could become the most powerful demon of all. He would then be able to defeat his enemies with the greatest of ease.

"You are a fool," the demon's teacher said. "Shiva will never give you the power that you want, if you tell him that you intend to wage war and destroy all who displease you."

But the warning only meant that Bhasmasura at once lost his temper - demons generally do, and Bhasmasura was certainly a demon with no self-control, nor any respect for teachers and elders. So he gave the poor man a severe thrashing!

"Bhasmasura, some day you will surely destroy yourself!" groaned the teacher, but this time he spoke very softly to himself.

Bhasmasura set about his task with real dedication. He was determined to get the absent-minded and forgetful god to notice him, even if it took a lifetime to do so! He was going to work his way into Shiva's good books! From then onwards, it seemed that Shiva had no more loyal devotee than the demon Bhasmasura. He was forever fasting and meditating, picking flowers for Parvati and dancing attendance on her, even finding the choicest grass and fruits for feeding Nandi, Shiva's pet bull!

At last his efforts were rewarded. One day a smiling Shiva stood before him. "I am well pleased with you, Bhasmasura. Ask for any wish and you shall have it."

"O generous one," said Bhasmasura, "grant that whoever's head I touch will be turned to ashes straight away!"

"So be it," pronounced Shiva, still smiling.

But a dreadful pride instantly welled up in the demon.

"Now I am the most powerful demon in the universe," he told himself. With no thought of gratitude, he decided that the very first victim of his new power would be Shiva himself! If he destroyed Shiva, Bhasmasura's power would be proven beyond doubt and all would fear him.

"Lord, if your gift is truly effective allow me to test it on your head," said Bhasmasura arrogantly, advancing one powerful hand toward's Shiva's matted locks!

The god stepped back in horror. Shiva's pet snake, wrapped around his neck, hissed at the approaching demon. Still Bhasmasura advanced, a nasty grin about his fanged mouth. Shiva hesitated no longer. The great god turned and fled!

Over hills and fields, through forests and narrow streets, Shiva fled for a day and a night with the ferocious demon hot on his trail. Tired of running, Shiva at last escaped the demon's attention for a moment and hid himself in a rubbish tip on the outskirts of a town! It did not immediately occur to Bhasmasura that the great god would be hiding himself, or be covered by filth and dirt. So he paused to consider where Shiva might be.

Now, when Shiva is in trouble, Vishnu, the Preserver, usually appears. In this instance he had observed all that had taken place. With the great Shiva, lord of Destruction, hiding in a smelly rubbish dump, Vishnu decided that it was time that he came to the rescue.

So Vishnu disguised himself as a beautiful dancing girl and called out to Bhasmasura. "Why is a handsome fellow like you wandering about in a dirty smelly place? Come away with me. Let us drink and be merry!"

The demon was so enchanted by the beauty of the dancing girl that he forgot about Shiva. He was highly flattered that she found him handsome. He followed her to an inn where she gave him plenty to drink while she danced for him. Bhasmasura was soon quite drunk. Demons have no self-control about these things.

Now the dancing girl began to tease him.

"Come and dance with me," she invited.

The clumsy giant got up and began to stagger about.

"No, no. You are not dancing properly!" cried the lovely maiden. "Let me show you how. Just follow my movements!"

Her brightly coloured skirt swirled around as she twirled on her toes. Bhasmasura too turned around, to copy her. The dance of the drunken demon must have been quite a sight! "Now put your foot there, an arm akimbo at your waist as you jump! It is such fun!" she laughed. "Now raise your hand as I do . . ."

This was the end of Bhasmasura, as you may have guessed. Vishnu, as the dancing girl, had placed a hand on his head. The foolish demon copied him. Bhasmasura turned himself into ashes!

The Dove and the Hawk

INDRA, the rain-giver and king of the gods, and his twin Agni, the red god of Fire, once had a friendly argument.

"Raja Shibi is so noble that he deserves to live in heaven. He is truly godlike in his compassion," said Agni.

"No man can be so perfect," argued Indra. "This king is in the habit of feeding you lots of butter - no wonder you are all buttered up and think him wonderful!" Indra laughed at his own silly joke. He knew that when sacrifices were offered to the gods, men would pour butter into the sacrificial fire and his brother would greedily lick it up with many flickering tongues. Fire was the medium that carried all sacrifices up to heaven.

"No, no! That is not the case. I am only repeating about Raja Shibi what all the world already says. His kindness has to be seen to be believed! Shibi is a king among kings!"

"Very well," agreed Indra. "Let us do just that, let us go down to earth and see for ourselves!"

Each day Raja Shibi used to sit in his court for a while. He believed that it was his kingly duty to act as a judge and listen to any complaints. His judgements were always praised for their wisdom.

One day while Shibi looked around the courtroom wondering who might come, seeking justice, a little white dove fluttered in through an open window. It flew straight towards him and fell exhausted into his lap! The king gently lifted the bird in his hand.

"Poor little dove," said Shibi softly and stroked the trembling feathery body. "How tired and frightened you are! Do not worry. No one shall harm you in my palace."

No sooner had he spoken than a large brown hawk swooped down and settled on a cushion by the king. Raja Shibi felt the dove shiver violently at the sight of the fierce bird, and it hid its little white head under its wings.

"Raja Shibi!" rasped out the hawk, "You are holding what is mine. Give him up to me. This dove is my food, and I have taken the trouble to chase him across the sky. The wretched creature is now tired out and can fly no more. If you had not sheltered him, he would have fallen to the ground or slowed down and, in either event, I would have caught him."

"Have compassion on him," said Shibi. "Let him live. Hunting is so cruel!"

"You talk of compassion, king!" said the hawk angrily. "Where is your compassion for me? I am very hungry. Humans hunt for pleasure but I only hunt for food. Is this room not supposed to be your hall of justice? Where is your justice then? That is my meal and you are cheating me of it."

"You are right," said Raja Shibi with a sigh. "I should consider your welfare too. But I cannot give up this dove when it has come to me for protection. But you shall not go hungry. This little dove is a poor meal. Wait, and I will order food to be brought for you."

"That dove is my food," insisted the hawk, "and you are wasting my time. Soon I will faint with hunger. Is this what you want? The only food I'll take is rich raw meat. It must be as fresh as the flesh of this living dove and weigh at least as much. If this bird means so much to you, why not give me your flesh to eat? Only then will I be satisfied. And hurry, or give up my rightful prey to me."

Raja Shibi thanked the hawk for his suggestion. He placed the little dove on a pair of scales and then, to the horror of his ministers, with his sharp sword he cut off some of the flesh from his left arm to weigh it on the scales. But his flesh made little impression on the scales. So he cut off the whole arm. It still did not seem to weigh as much as the dove!

"More!" cried the hawk, "I must have more flesh!"

"Your Majesty," said the Chief Minister, "this is madness! Some sorcery is afoot. These birds will destroy you, if you let them!"

But Shibi asked him to remain calm. "It is better that I die than that I should fail in my duty! I must save this dove as well as keep my bargain with the hawk." He continued to slice off his flesh and put it on the scales.

Weak with loss of blood, Shibi realised that nothing at all seemed to make a difference to the scales which still hung heavy on the side with the little dove. At last the king said, "Eat all of my body, hawk, and spare this dove."

Immediately a heavenly music sounded in the hall and perfumed flower petals rained down upon the king and the birds. His wounds instantly healed and his body was whole again. Looking up, Shibi saw that in place of the hawk stood the splendid form of Indra and the dove was none other than fiery Agni. Both gods looked lovingly at him.

"Truly, Raja Shibi, you are the most merciful of men. Such compassion is worthy of heaven. When the time comes, I will gladly welcome you to my heavenly kingdom of Indraloka," promised Indra.

Both the gods blessed the king and then vanished.

The Dwarf's Three Steps

THE greatest of the demons, the mighty Bali, ruled over Patal, the dreadful and violent underworld of the demons. For a demon he had many good qualities. He was known for his generosity, honesty, courage and great feats of strength. Also Bali's devotion to duty and to God won him immense favour. The demons were his loyal subjects and swore to follow him to the ends of the universe if need be. But, for all his virtues, Bali remained a demon, and two of his greatest faults were pride and greed.

One day Bali summoned Shukracharya, the Guru, or teacher, of the demons, to his throne room. Shukracharya was a powerful and cunning magician, who, it was said, could see into the future. He found Bali stomping about the marble hall, making the thick round pillars shake.

Bali came straight to the point. "By your blessings, Guru, I rule over all of Patal. But this is not enough and I am bored. My demons too will soon be bored. They are all good fighters and I, their king, must lead them into more and more battles. What should I do?"

The lean and white-bearded teacher was thoughtful for a while. Then he said, "Your Majesty, you still have to conquer the world from which I come, the world of humans. It is a world that demons have often entered to loot its treasures and bring them back to Patal. That is why this underworld is so wealthy and your palace glitters with gold and jewels. Yet the foolish humans go on working and producing more wealth! It would not be difficult for a mighty warrior like yourself to bring their world, too, under your rule once and for all. But you must control your demons on Earth. The human world is too precious to be destroyed. Nor must its people all be killed. You need them to work for you!"

In this way Shukracharya counselled the king.

Nor did it take long for Bali and his hordes of demons to overrun the Earth. Many earthly kings feared him so much that they laid down their arms without a struggle. Bali was generous enough to return their thrones to these rulers, insisting only that they must view him as their emperor and make him costly gifts in food, wealth and humans whenever he demanded them. Those kings who were foolhardy enough to fight against him were quickly killed, and replaced by Bali with his chosen demons who governed these lands for him. But Bali could not always control his demons and they sometimes did very wicked things. The gods watched from Heaven in horror.

But Bali, Lord of Patal and of Earth, was still not satisfied.

"Guru, unless I can bring Heaven, too, under my rule, there will still be those who will say that Indra, king of the gods, is mightier than Bali."

Shukracharya shook his head. "My Lord, your armies overran the Earth and the gods did not lift a finger. Perhaps they were afraid. But remember that the gods sometimes allow wicked things to happen, only to see how far such wickedness will go. Do not tempt fate by attacking Heaven. Spend some time now establishing your rule on Earth. Spend time in Patal, too, with your wives and children. What does it matter what people say about Indra? Is it not enough to know in your heart of hearts that you are his superior?"

But Bali would not agree. Seeing that the demon-king was determined to battle with the gods, his teacher gave his assent, saying, "Be victorious yet again, Lord Bali. May you fly your flag over Indra's palace!"

The gods, led by Indra, on his magnificent white elephant Airavata, were lined up to give battle when Bali and his demons stormed into Indraloka, Indra's heaven. The fighting was fierce but the gods were no match for Bali. At last Indra saw his army scattered and exhausted, while the terrible figure of Bali strode towards him with sword upraised. "I cannot be captured and dragged down to Patal in chains for the demons to mock me," thought Indra. As a god, he could not die, in battle or in any other way. So with a heavy heart he gave the order and Airavata, the winged elephant, swiftly fled the battlefield.

Bali laughed to see Indra disappearing into the clouds. Now *he* was the new king of Heaven!

Indra's palace was the grandest building that Bali had ever seen, surpassing even his wildest dreams. He knew he would never discover all its fascinating treasures or learn all of its secrets. Mindful of his teacher's advice, Bali was most respectful to the beautiful goddesses who lived in it, and asked the talented musicians, singers and dancers to continue as though there had been no change in ruler.

The overjoyed demons hailed Bali as king of the Three Worlds of Patal, Earth, and Indraloka.

Meanwhile Indra and some of the other gods who had fled appealed to Vishnu, the great God, for help. Indra spoke for them all. "O Beautiful One! Protector of the Universe, Saviour of all Creation, save us now! The demon Bali has captured the Earth and Heaven! Even now he occupies my throne! He has overturned nature and caused the gods to flee! Surely he carries the mark of your protection to have got away with such deeds! It is your responsibility to restore order to the Three Worlds. The innocent gods and humans are paying the price of this upstart demon's greed and pride. Only you can help us. The demons are your creation, but so are the gods and humans. Do not abandon us to the demons!"

Vishnu, ever gracious, received his visitors kindly, but he was not particularly disturbed to think of their disgrace. It did Indra and the other gods no harm for their pride to be humbled now and then!

"Never despise the lowly demon," said Vishnu. "Goodness and a noble nature may be found in Patal too! This demon Bali is one of the best! It is his own human and godlike nature which has attracted him to both Earth and Heaven. He has no doubt committed many sins, but know also that this very demon has been my devotee all his life! There are few on Earth or even Indraloka who can match his devotion to God. That devotion is the source of all his power. A true devotee offers himself and all his actions to me. So I must bear the burden of his sins."

But Vishnu agreed that the demon-king could not be allowed to cause further havoc. He reassured the gods that both they and the people on Earth would soon be free, and he himself would deal with Bali.

So Vishnu changed himself into a very young dwarf, wearing the simple orange robe of the holy man and carrying a begging bowl. In this disguise he appeared before Bali's palace. As soon as they spotted him some of the demons started to push him from one to the other, teasing him because of his small size. But they soon tired of this when they found that their victim did not complain.

A demon, guarding the palace, now called out to him. "What do you want; are you not afraid of us?"

"I am a wandering holy man," replied the young dwarf. "I beg from place to place. Raja Bali is famous for his charity, so I came to beg from him. Please take me to him."

"Yes," thought the guard, "our king is both religious and charitable. He will reward me for bringing this holy dwarf to his presence." So he agreed to lead him to Bali.

The king was with Shukracharya when the guard informed him that a holy youth waited for his charity.

"Your Majesty, I beg you not to see this beggar!" advised the guru of the demons in some alarm. "Something tells me that this is no ordinary beggar and the meeting will only do you harm. Send him away."

But Bali would not listen and went to the courtyard to greet the holy man. He looked down at the dwarf, from his smiling eyes and bright intelligent face to his dusty bare feet. "You are most welcome, man of God," said the king respectfully. "Let me wash your holy feet."

Bali lifted a water pitcher to pour water over the dwarf's tiny feet, but to his surprise no water came out of the spout. The dwarf, who was of course Vishnu, knew that Bali's guru had used his magic to hide himself in the pitcher and it was he who was blocking the spout! Since he could not stop the king from seeing the visitor, cunning Shukracharya had decided to hide in the pitcher and look through the spout to see if he could identify the dwarf.

"The spout is blocked," the dwarf said, "but this reed will soon unblock it!" Picking up a reed, he pushed it into the spout of the pitcher. His sharp ears heard a tiny cry of pain. The reed had poked the eye of the teacher-magician who now drew back, unblocking the spout.

"That's better!" said Bali, unaware of what had happened. He bathed the dwarf's feet and wiped them dry.

"Now, what charity do you wish of me?" asked the king.

"Lord of the Three Worlds, I want only as much land as I can cover in three steps."

"So be it," agreed Bali, wondering at this strange request. Three strides taken by this tiny youth, really could not amount to much!

But the dwarf now grew and grew and grew. He was no longer a dwarf, but a giant. The giant continued to grow until his size was beyond imagination. With one step he covered the Earth and with the other Heaven.

"Indraloka and Earth are now mine," said the beggar, "but you have promised me another step. Where else may I place my foot?"

"My guru warned me. You are certainly no ordinary beggar," said Bali. "But the only land left depends on whether you have legs left to measure a third step."

The giant did have a third leg! It now grew from his navel! "Where may I place my foot to claim my third step?" he thundered.

Raja Bali now knew that this dwarf-giant-beggar was none other than his beloved Lord Vishnu. How wonderful that God should come to his door to beg! He knelt humbly before the visitor and removed his crown. "My Lord, place your foot upon my head," he said with devotion as he bowed his head.

Vishnu's third foot gently but surely came down on the demon's head. It pushed Bali deeper and deeper down to the depths of the world of demons, Patal.

Thus Vishnu saved mankind and the gods and also made Bali extremely happy and blessed by placing his foot on the demon's head. Bali was now content to rule over Patal and leave both Earth and Heaven alone.

Krishna - Man and God

KRISHNA was the noble king of Dwarka nearly four thousand years ago. He was famous for his wisdom - a philosopher-king they called him. He ruled with both justice and mercy. Many people sought his advice and he never turned away a single person who sincerely asked for his help. For all his royal dignity and many kingly accomplishments, Krishna always remembered his humble upbringing in the forest of Brindaban where, as a boy he had looked after his foster parents' cattle and played with the other cowherds. Although he now wore a golden crown, he still sported a peacock feather in his curly black hair to remind him of those carefree days, and was known on occasions to put away his rich clothes and become again the simple fun-loving youth when his childhood friends called on him. Krishna was, in fact, the great god Vishnu, born on Earth just as he had been born many times before - for a special purpose.

Naturally Krishna was very popular. Even people who did not get along with each other would still be proud to count him as a mutual friend. The Pandava princes, for instance, who were the five sons of King Pandu, became good friends of Krishna. Closest to him, among them, was the third brother, Arjuna, said to be the finest archer in all the world. But Krishna was friendly too with their cousins and sworn enemies, the hundred Kaurava brothers whose greed for more power and territory had led them to make many attempts on the lives of their five cousins. Through trickery and deceit, the Kauravas succeeded more than once in having the Pandavas banished to the forests for several years while they seized the whole kingdom for themselves.

You may be sure that the five princes had many strange adventures while they were exiled in the forest. One of the most wonderful of these was how they came to win the hand in marriage of the beautiful princess Draupadi. Yes, one wife for five brothers! It was in the process of winning Draupadi during their first exile that the Pandavas met Krishna, and it was the start of a lifelong friendship.

In ancient India it was the custom for highborn ladies to choose their own husbands at a special ceremony where all their suitors would be present. To help them make their choice the suitors were often set difficult or dangerous tasks so that they could prove their worth. The eventual winner would then hope to marry the princess whose ceremony it was.

Draupadi, daughter of King Drupada of Panchala, was as virtuous as she was beautiful. She had great strength of character too, and from her childhood had worshipped God with great devotion. When it was time for her to choose a husband, her father issued invitations far and

wide for suitors to come to a ceremony and prove
themselves worthy to marry his daughter. Many were the
princes who were eager to win Draupadi as a bride.
Among them was Duryodhana, the eldest of the Kaurava
brothers, and also, disguised as beggars, were the five
Pandava brothers. Sitting among the family guests with
King Drupada and his lovely daughter was Krishna, the
king of Dwarka.

The task set seemed impossible to most of the suitors.
They were handed a great bow and asked to string it and
shoot five arrows through the hole in a revolving disk at
a tiny target shaped like a fish, which they could only see
as a reflection in the water of a well. One by one the
distinguished suitors tried, but walked away defeated.
Most of them could not even bend the mighty bow, let
alone string it. To fail like this was a great blow to
Duryodhana's pride.

"No human can perform this task!" he complained.
"At this rate the lady will have none left to marry her."

Arjuna now stepped forward to lift the bow, but was
met with an outcry. Duryodhana and his friends did not
think it right that a beggar should enter the contest. But
Draupadi had noticed that the five beggars were handsome men whose ragged clothes did not hide their heroic
build. She willingly gave her agreement for Arjuna to take
part in the contest. Nor was Krishna fooled. As soon as he
saw the five beggars he guessed that these must be the
princes in exile, disguised to avoid detection by
Duryodhana and his spies, for the story of the five
Pandava brothers who had lost their kingdom and wan-
dered in the forest was well known.

Krishna spoke softly to pacify some of the angry
suitors. "Since the fair Draupadi agrees, let this man be

put to the test, gentle princes, kings and friends. A man's true nature proclaims whether he is a prince or a beggar. Do not judge anyone by outward appearances."

Arjuna looked into the kindly eyes of the king of Dwarka and sent him a silent message of thanks. Then, with a prayer to Vishnu in his heart, he picked up the giant bow, bent it and easily placed the string on it. As the crowd gasped in amazement, for no one had so far succeeded in stringing the bow, Arjuna fitted an arrow to the string, lifted the bow above his head and looking steadfastly at the reflection in the well water he let fly at the target. His arrow winged its way through the tiny hole in the revolving disk and hit the fish hanging high above. Without stopping Arjuna shot another arrow and then another, till all five arrows had hit their target and the bright metal fish fell to the ground.

Arjuna's triumph was complete when Draupadi put her flower garland around his neck and chose him as her husband. So at the end of the day it was the beggar-prince, accompanied by his four brothers, who led away the famous princess, while Duryodhana returned to his own capital city of Hastinapura in disgust.

The Pandava princes were in the habit of sharing everything with each other. Living in the forest as they did, with their widowed mother, Kunti, they all depended on Arjuna's skill with bow and arrow to provide their food. Sometimes it was venison and sometimes a rabbit. On this day when Arjuna called out to his mother to see what prize his archery had brought home, Kunti did not turn around to look. Instead, she said, with an absent-minded air, "Oh good! Of course you will share with your brothers, as usual!"

Now, a mother's word is a command for a dutiful son.

Draupadi and the Pandava brothers were horrified, as was Kunti herself when she realised what she had said, but they all knew that they were now bound by honour to share Draupadi as their common wife. At this moment Krishna appeared. He had secretly followed them to the cottage deep in the forest.

"Do not worry, daughter," he comforted the princess. "It is your destiny to have the five noblest men any girl could want for your husbands. You are the most fortunate of women. Your happiness in marriage will be multiplied five times! I know that you will be able to manage this situation."

With a mischievous smile the laughter-loving Krishna showed Draupadi his divine form. "Do you remember your daily prayer to me, these many years? It was: 'Lord, may I marry the noblest man in all the world.' You repeated it five times each day. Princess, your prayer is granted." Draupadi trembled to see the shining gracious form of the beloved Vishnu of her prayers.

This was a great spiritual moment. Vishnu, she now knew, was on Earth as the philosopher-king, Krishna.

Krishna blessed Draupadi and Kunti and her sons, promising them his protection in the difficult times to come.

Krishna's prophecy came true. So greatly did the brothers love and respect one another and Draupadi, their queen, that this unusual marriage worked perfectly. They all lived together in peace and joy.

But hard times were soon upon them. When the years of their exile ended, the Pandava brothers returned to their kingdom. But the evil Duryodhana drove them out once again. He even dared to do a most insulting thing. He sent one of his younger brothers to fetch Draupadi to his court.

The Kaurava prince dragged the unwilling lady by her beautiful long hair, until she stood in the palace court of Hastinapura surrounded by the jeering Kauravas. Wishing to humiliate his Pandava cousins through their queen, the eldest of the Kaurava brothers gave the order for her to be disrobed. Rough hands pulled at Draupadi's sari.

Draupadi stood tall and proud in her grief and anger. She closed her eyes and called upon Krishna to rescue her honour. Everyone present at the court of Hastinapura witnessed a miracle that day. Round and round the lady turned and metre upon metre of shimmering silk sari cascaded onto the marble floor. It seemed as if Draupadi wore a never ending sari, and all present rubbed their eyes as one colourful sari seemed to merge with yet another. Draupadi alone with closed eyes could see the beautiful form of Vishnu in the hall. She remembered how, in her childhood play as she dressed her dolls in saris, she had always thought of him. "Here are those same saris now," said the god, "increased many times over. Such is the power of prayer."

Finding that they were unable to disrobe Draupadi, the Kauravas gave up their shameful attempt.

Driven out by their cousins for the second time, the Pandavas went into exile for thirteen years, accompanied by Draupadi. Once more they lived a simple life in the forest where many gods, demons, and wise men, came their way. But they were not forgotten by their own world either, for their powerful friend, Krishna, the king of Dwarka, would sometimes visit them. They developed great faith in Krishna and trusted him to guide their lives in all matters.

When the long years of their second exile finally ended, the Pandavas found the Kauravas once again unwilling to return their kingdom to them. Krishna himself acted as a go-between and pleaded for the five brothers. He reminded Duryodhana that he had made a solemn promise, in public, to restore the kingdom to the Pandavas at the end of thirteen years. But the Kaurava prince was not a man of honour and did not hesitate to break his word. Krishna knew that war would break out between the cousins if the Pandavas continued to be cheated of their inheritance, and that many thousands would die. In the cause of peace, and to give the Kauravas every chance to undo their wrong, Krishna made one last effort.

"Duryodhana, if you will not return them half the kingdom along with the beautiful city of Indraprastha which your cousins built from the wilderness, at least give them five villages to rule over."

But the greedy Kauravas refused to accept even this.

War was inevitable. The Pandavas knew that they had to fight for their kingdom even if they died in the attempt. Many were the kings and nobles who came to ally themselves with the Pandavas in order to help them in their just cause. But many who were friends and relatives of both sides, felt painfully divided in their loyalty. Some simply gave their support to whichever side was the first to ask for it. This was the case for instance with Drona, the warrior and teacher of both the Pandavas and the Kauravas in their youth. Drona had always tried to treat the princes in his charge with equal fairness. He had watched them growing up together: Yudhishtira the just, eldest of the sons of king Pandu, who showed all the early signs of becoming a great king; Bhima the strong, the second Pandava, who was a giant of a man; and Arjuna, that prince among archers who had become Drona's favourite pupil. Yet it was Duryodhana who first requested Drona's help in the great war to come and Drona agreed to become one of the Kaurava captains.

Duryodhana, on behalf of the Kauravas, and Arjuna, on behalf of the Pandavas, came to ask Krishna for help. Duryodhana arrived first and was told by servants that their royal master was asleep. But he was not going to risk losing Krishna's help, so he entered the bedroom and sat down in a grand throne-like chair by Krishna's head. When Arjuna arrived he learnt that his cousin was waiting in the bedroom for Krishna to wake up, so he too went to the bedroom but sat down more humbly at the foot of Krishna's bed. When the king of Dwarka awoke he was glad to see Arjuna, for it was the Pandava prince that he saw first.

But Duryodhana quickly pressed his claim: "I was here first and so surely it is I who should have your help!"

Speaking very calmly Krishna said that both had equal claims to seek his help, Arjuna whom he had seen first, and Duryodhana who had arrived first. "You must choose," he said, "the kind of help you want. On the one hand there is my vast army of trained soldiers with weapons, horses, and elephants. Whichever one of you wants this is welcome to it. On the other hand there is only myself. If one of you should choose me I will help you, but I shall not myself use any weapon in the war to come."

The two cousins quickly made up their minds, each according to his nature. For Duryodhana it was obvious that the powerful army was worth having on his side in the battles to come, an unarmed Krishna could in no way match so powerful a force. Arjuna was equally sure that nothing in the world mattered except that God should be on his side. There were moments when the pure-hearted prince recognised that Krishna was really God, and in his mercy he appeared to Arjuna as a loving human friend and wise counsellor. How it came to be that Krishna was both God and man, Arjuna did not stop to puzzle.

"Krishna, you are all that I want," said the Pandava hero.

"So be it," declared Krishna, and the two cousins left him, each feeling well satisfied.

True to his promise, Krishna sent his army, fully equipped, to swell the numbers of the Kaurava force, while he himself, carrying no weapons, became Arjuna's charioteer.

On the battlefield of Kurukshetra the two armies faced each other, and before the battle began Arjuna looked across to the opposite side where he saw many friends and relatives, people he loved and admired, now ranged against him. A terrible sorrow overcame him and he felt that he could not wage war on such men as these. If he won, it would only be by killing those he held dear, people such as his beloved teacher Drona, and such a victory would not be worth having.

Krishna realised the confusion and doubt that gripped Arjuna's mind. Now more than ever did Arjuna need the guidance of his friend, the philosopher-king. Luckily, Krishna's words of wisdom at this critical time have come down to us as the *Bhagavad Gita*, which means the "Song of God". In eloquent words Krishna reminded his friend of where his duty lay.

"Man must do his duty without thinking of any reward," taught Krishna.

Arjuna understood that his duty as a prince lay in fighting evil, not because he hoped to win, but because evil must never be tolerated. He learnt that man was more than just a body, he was also a soul which could never die.

Arjuna also discovered that Krishna had, like him, been born to fulfil a special purpose.

"Age after age I am born on this earth, to protect the good and to destroy the evildoer. Whenever the conditions call for my presence in the world, then I am born to carry out my mission," was the gracious promise of Krishna.

While the two armies waited, still and tense, as though frozen in time, Arjuna had a glimpse of Krishna's true nature. Where a moment ago stood his trusted charioteer, Arjuna now saw the mind-shattering form of God as master of the universe. The two great armies, the battlefield, he himself, the universe, nothing existed except in God. Awestruck by this mighty vision the Pandava hero turned away his face.

"Lord, protect me!" he cried. "Show me once more the human form of my charioteer and friend."

The smiling face of Krishna appeared before him again, a peacock feather in his dark hair. His moment of rare knowledge had brought Arjuna very close to God, and now with renewed strength of purpose he lifted his famous bow, Gandiva, to challenge the enemy.

For eighteen days the battle raged and the field of Kurukshetra ran red with blood. Few were left alive on either side. Krishna had foreseen this terrible destruction and had cast his protection over the Pandava brothers, all of whom survived the war and won, for Yudhishtira, the eldest of them, the combined kingdom of the Kauravas and the Pandavas.

One other family survived the slaughter, thanks to the mercy of God. A little lapwing had built a nest of grass and twigs right in the middle of the battlefield. The nest with its tiny eggs lay hidden in the taller grass but once the

battle began it seemed certain that it would be trampled under the feet of soldiers, horses, and elephants, or crushed beneath chariot wheels. But even when the war conches blew, and the earth shook as the armies prepared to do battle, the little bird refused to leave her nest helpless and unprotected. Her tiny despairing cries were heard by Krishna who left his chariot and followed the sound until he found the lapwing and her nest.

"Little mother," he said in his gentlest voice, "your devotion to your family is the highest form of love. You and your innocent little ones have no part in this terrible war. You will not suffer because of it."

Krishna blessed the bird and her still unhatched brood. Then he picked up an elephant bell that had fallen on the battlefield. These large bronze bells were proudly worn on a chain round the necks of war elephants in ancient India. Very carefully Krishna covered the lapwing and her nest with the great bell. In this way they were kept safe for the whole of that fearsome battle.

Thousands of years have passed since these events took place. The modern city of Meerut now stands where the Kauravas once had their capital city, Hastinapura. Over the ruins of the proud Pandava city of Indraprastha flies the national flag of India, for this site is now Delhi, the country's historic capital. The field of Kurukshetra lies still and bare with only the wind blowing through the tall grass, but if you listen carefully you may just hear the happy song of lapwings drifting on the breeze. The noble deeds of the Pandavas live on in the memory, and the inspiring song of Krishna uplifts the hearts of men. God's mercy continues to protect the world, even the tiniest bird.

Bhima and the Monkey's Tail

DHRITARASHTRA and Pandu were brothers who were kings in north India hundreds of years ago. Dhritarashtra, the elder brother, had a hundred sons by his queen, Rani Gandhari. These sons were often referred to as the Kauravas.

Pandu had only five sons. But these five, often called the Pandavas, were not really Pandu's sons. They were gifts of the gods. Pandu and his queens, Rani Kunti and Rani Madri, had no children because Pandu had been cursed so that he could never father children of his own. Yet they all longed for children. Kunti, therefore, used a special prayer on behalf of herself and Madri so that they might both have sons born of the gods. These sons were thought of as Pandu's children.

Dharma, the god of Justice, came first to Kunti, the elder queen and fathered a son who grew up to be the noble prince Yudhishtira. To Kunti also appeared the god of the Wind, Vayu. Their son became the strong man, Bhima. Indra, Vayu's brother who is king of all the gods, gave Kunti another son, Arjuna, who became the famous archer-prince. The shining Ashwini twins, the healers of heaven, came to Madri, Pandu's second wife, and gave her the handsome twins Nakula and Sahadeva.

When Raja Pandu died, the five Pandava brothers were brought up at Hastinapura, with their hundred Kaurava cousins. The Pandavas soon realised that their cousins were greedy, jealous and dishonest, doing their utmost to make life unpleasant for the five brothers. The Kaurava princes did not openly express their enmity because they were afraid of Bhima, whose immense size and strength seemed superhuman. As time went on, the Kauravas plotted to kill their five cousins, but all their attempts failed. They did, however, succeed in getting the Pandavas and Rani Kunti banished to the forests.

Bhima's strength was very useful in the forest. When building a shelter or clearing a path, he would tear down branches and even trees with his bare hands. Vasuki, king of the Nagas, or snakes, was so impressed by Bhima's strength and generous nature, that he blessed him by multiplying his natural strength. So Bhima was said to have the strength of ten thousand elephants, and everyone knows that the elephant is the strongest of beasts!

Sometimes when his brothers and mother were weary with walking in the forest, Bhima would lift them all up and carry them together! He also fought many wild beasts and monsters in their defence.

But brave and good though he was, Bhima began to feel very proud of his great strength, and to consider that he was a greater hero than his brothers. "I am the strongest man the world has ever seen," he thought to himself. "Surely even the gods cannot match my strength!"

One day Bhima set off to hunt for food. He walked along a path that was scarcely wide enough for his large body. Suddenly he saw a thin shabby monkey lying stretched across the path. In his hurry Bhima had almost stepped on it. The monkey's eyes were closed and it was snoring gently. The straggly brown tail swished lightly on the ground, as though the monkey was dreaming.

"What a nuisance!" thought the prince. The monkey was clearly extremely old and it would be most disrespectful to step on it or even to step over it.

"Ho, monkey!" called out Bhima. "Get up and move aside for me to pass."

But the monkey did not budge. Indeed, its snores grew louder. This really irritated Bhima so he shouted at the monkey, "Get up, you moth-eaten bag of bones! I know you must be awake. How dare you block my path!"

The monkey opened one eye. "What's that you say?" it drawled lazily.

"Up with you and out of my way," Bhima thundered in a rage, "before I strangle your skinny neck! I am Bhima the terrible Pandava and you are blocking my path at your peril, you miserable wretch!"

"Ah, great one, please forgive me," said the monkey. "I shake with fear at your mighty wrath." But its eyes glistened with mischief and it made no effort to raise itself.

Bhima could not believe this was happening to him! He stamped on the ground, causing a minor earthquake!

"Noble prince, have mercy!" whined the monkey, in its mocking voice. "Old age has made me hard of hearing and extremely feeble. I fear I have lost all power of movement. I haven't even the strength to move my poor tail out of your royal path. Please forgive my weakness. But your mighty arms could easily lift me clear of your path, if you could bear to touch a shabby monkey like me!"

"Lift you in my arms, monkey?" roared the prince. "I shall grab that scruffy tail and whirl you about my head before you come crashing down to meet your doom!"

Bhima bent down to grasp the wispy tail. But in some strange way it seemed too heavy to lift. He looked suspiciously at the old monkey's face, but innocent brown eyes stared back at him. He tried again with redoubled energy, but again he failed. He panted and perspired. The mighty Pandava, Bhima, was not one to give up easily, but the enormous weight of the monkey's tail was like that of a solid mountain blocking his way. At last, exhausted, he gave up the attempt and stood up with his hands joined together in humility.

"I see now that you are mightier than myself, and I am ashamed of my previous boasting. Will you not tell me who you are, so that I may learn who has taught me a lesson in good manners?" he humbly asked.

The monkey sprang up with remarkable swiftness. In front of Bhima's astonished eyes it transformed itself. A tall and gleaming man-monkey with a strong curled tail and carrying a huge club over his muscular shoulder, faced him. Bhima knelt in wonder and worship.

"How blessed I am that you should appear before me! The stories of your marvellous strength are sung all over the land. Since childhood I have admired you and wished to be like you. Lord Rama's champion and friend, mighty Hanuman, you are the famous son of Vayu, the Wind. . ."

"And I am also your brother!" finished the smiling stranger. Bhima found himself lifted up by steely strong arms and given a mighty hug.

"Little brother," said Hanuman to the giant Bhima, "you have your duties here on earth, but our father, Vayu, and I always watch over you. I came to warn you that you will never face such a danger in battle or from your enemies, as that when your own strength began to change your noble character. Be your lovable self - simple, modest and gallant. Better to be loved for these qualities than feared for your strength."

The wise monkey and Bhima, both sons of Vayu, had much to say to each other at this first meeting. But finally they bade each other a fond farewell. Hanuman then vanished but left behind his war-club as a gift for Bhima.

Yudhishtira's Journey

I N THE terrible battle of Kurukshetra, between the
Pandavas and the Kauravas, countless people died.
Not only did all hundred of the Kaurava brothers
lose their lives, but all the young sons of the five Pandava
princes were killed too, including Abhimanyu, the son of
Arjuna, the third Pandava prince. Abhimanyu had gone
into battle despite the pleas of his wife, who was expecting
a baby. Brave Abhimanyu never returned, but his son
Parikshit was eventually born.

The outcome of the battle was that the good Pandavas
won back the kingdom which was rightfully theirs. So
Parikshit was brought up as a prince of Hastinapura. His
now childless uncles, Yudhishtira, Bhima, Nakula and
Sahadeva, treated him as Arjuna did, like their own son.

Yudhishtira, the eldest Pandava, became the new ruler.
He proved to be an excellent king. Under him the kingdom enjoyed peace and prosperity, the people loved him
and even his enemies respected him and called him
"Yudhishtira the Just".

One day Yudhishtira heard that his friend, Krishna the

Raja of Dwarka, and all his tribe, the Yadavas, had been killed. The court was plunged into grief at this tragic news.

"Alas, Krishna! You were always our guide," thought the king. "Without your support we would never have regained our land. With you gone, what a poor and dull place this world now seems!"

Yudhishtira prayed and fasted. Then he called his brothers and Draupadi who was wife to all five of them.

"Life and its pleasures have lost all meaning for me. I wish to spend my remaining time on earth in prayer and pilgrimage. So it is time to say goodbye to you all."

Yudhishtira asked Bhima, the second brother, to take his crown. But Bhima refused. Instead he announced his intention of following his elder brother's example. Indeed they all insisted on accompanying Yudhishtira.

"Some years ago our mother, Rani Kunti, also left the palace and went into the forest where she died," said Arjuna. "You are not the only one to feel that you have lived a long and full life. We too have aged with you. It is right that we now follow the time-honoured custom of spending our old age in living very simply and worshipping God. Going on pilgrimage is a way of worship that will suit us well. Let us all go with you, brother. We have always been together and shared everything, so many hardships, battles, joys and sorrows. Let us also share this last great adventure together, the journey to God."

Rani Draupadi also pleaded to go with them.

So it was agreed that young Parikshit, grandson of Arjuna, should become Raja of Hastinapura. The five brothers and Draupadi blessed him. They exchanged their rich clothes and jewels for the humble clothes of forest-dwellers and set off on foot for the Himalaya mountains, their minds fixed on God.

Some of the holiest places lie high near the mountain peaks and are difficult to reach. But the six pilgrims kept climbing ever higher. They visited many holy places and then came to a great mountain. As they began to go up this mountain, a little black mongrel joined their procession.

The way was very hard. One by one Yudhishtira's companions: Draupadi, Sahadeva, Nakula, Arjuna, Bhima, all fell and died. As each one fell, the others carried on. At last only Yudhishtira and the dog were left. But Yudhishtira kept calm. "All who are born must die," he reasoned. "God alone endures. He must have willed their deaths."

Yudhishtira continued climbing, until he reached the summit. There he saw the splendid figure of Indra standing by a golden flying chariot.

"Congratulations, Yudhishtira, noblest of men!" said the king of the gods. "Your goodness has so impressed the gods that I have come to carry you to my heaven, Indraloka, even though you are still in a human body."

Yudhishtira thanked the god for his great honour. Then he looked down at the dog which had followed him for so many days and nights.

"This dog is my faithful companion, Lord Indra. Please let him also enter your chariot," he begged.

But Indra would not hear of it. "Certainly not! No dirty dog may enter my chariot. Nor will I allow any dog in Indraloka."

He gave Yudhishtira a choice. He had to give up one or the other - either heaven or the dog.

Yudhishtira did not hesitate. "I will stay here with this dog," he said.

At once the dog changed into Dharma, god of Justice, and Yudhishtira's heavenly father! He smiled at him. "This was a test of your loyalty, and I am proud of you!"

Dharma and Indra flew the Pandava king to glorious Indraloka. It was a beautiful place but Yudhishtira could not find his loved ones anywhere. Instead, he saw his Kaurava cousins enjoying themselves in heaven! These were the evil men who had wronged him and his family!

"Why are Duryodhana and his brothers in heaven?" he demanded angrily. "Is this justice?"

But Dharma answered mildly, "My son, because you have entered heaven with a human body, you still feel such emotions as anger, which have no place here. To fit yourself for Indraloka, you must see all with the eye of love."

Dharma advised Yudhishtira that he should fly through hell in Indra's chariot for the briefest moment. "This will burn away any anger still left in you. But do not worry. At no time will the chariot stop in hell and nor will you see any of its ugliness."

"Lord, I will gladly enter hell, if it is for my good," declared the king.

He entered Indra's chariot again. At once it flew into the air. The next moment Yudhishtira realised that he was in complete darkness. There was a dreadful feeling about the place. Although he could see nothing, he sensed that all around him were many souls in terrible agony. His heart was filled with pity.

"This is a monstrous place," he thought and longed to be away from it.

"Ah, stop, my son!" called a pitiful voice. Surely it was not the voice of his mother, Kunti? If only he could exchange places with her!

"Brother, wait!" called a feeble voice which, with a shock, he recognised as mighty Bhima's.

"Noble brother!" cried Arjuna's voice. "Stay only a

moment longer! With you has entered such a pure fresh air that it eases our pain for a while."

"Beloved uncle, do not leave us!" called the boyish voice of Abhimanyu.

From the cries around him Yudhishtira realised that his wife Draupadi, his brothers and their sons, other family members and friends, were all here in hell.

"Oh, stop the chariot," cried Yudhishtira. "Lord, how terribly they are suffering!"

Dharma's voice answered him: "What did you expect? This is hell and those who are here are meant to suffer. But you need not suffer like them. Heaven is waiting for you. Your moment in hell is now over."

"No," said Yudhishtira. "I will stay here and share the sufferings of my loved ones. My place is with them. Do you, Lord, return to Indraloka without me."

The next moment, a wonderful light engulfed him. Yudhishtira looked around in wonder. How much more glorious was this place than the heaven he had first seen! Smiling Dharma and Indra stood on either side of him.

"This is not hell, Yudhishtira," said the god of Justice. "This place was always heaven! You have now passed your final test and are ready to join your dear ones."

Yudhishtira saw his heroic brothers, more splendid than he had ever seen them, Draupadi, more beautiful than ever. Kunti had such royal dignity! Other family members and friends also looked at him with love and joy.

"*Now* I am in heaven!" exclaimed Yudhishtira, rushing to embrace them.

Heaven was indeed a place of joy beyond compare, a place of love and beauty. "Welcome to Indraloka!" sang the gods and goddesses, coming forward to greet him. Yudhishtira had finally reached his journey's end.

Kunti's Secret Son

WHEN Kunti was a very young child, she was adopted by Kuntibhoja. Kuntibhoja loved the company of good and wise people and many such friends used to come to their house. Kunti was always most respectful to their guests and happy to help her father in serving them. "Kuntibhoja, your daughter is a jewel," praised many a visitor. "Daughter, may you be a mother of heroes!" was their blessing.

"Will I truly be a mother of heroes?" giggled the little girl one day. Durvasa, a wise old man who was visiting Kuntibhoja at the time, took her question seriously and decided to look into the future. He had practised yoga for many years, and had developed many strange powers. He saw now that when Kunti grew up she would marry a good king. But alas, her husband would be cursed and be unable to have any children!

"What can I do to help her?" Durvasa wondered, for he knew that what he had seen would be a great disappointment to the lovely child.

"Child," said Durvasa kindly, "you shall indeed be a mother of famous heroes. I will teach you a secret prayer which has a magical power. Whenever you recite this prayer and call to any god, that god will appear to you. You will immediately be blessed by the god with a son who will have some of his glory. But this prayer is for the purpose of having sons only, so mind how you use it!"

After Durvasa left, Kunti thought over what he had said. Could his words be true?

Early one morning Kunti got up and went to bathe in the river. As she came out of the water, dripping wet, a marvellous sunrise spread rosy streaks across the sky and was reflected in the river.

"O Sun-god, how beautiful you are!" thought Kunti. She felt like trying out her secret prayer and did so, without heeding Durvasa's warning to be careful.

At once a shining and splendid looking figure appeared in front of her. "Do not be afraid, dear Kunti. I am Surya, the Sun," said the god in his deep voice. "You have called me by the power of your prayer. I shall give you a glorious hero for your first born son."

Too late Kunti cried: "No, no! I want no child. I am still only a young girl myself. I am not even married. What will the world say if I should have a baby? No one will believe that you are the father. No one will want to marry me if I already have a child!"

But the children of gods are born instantly, so even as Kunti spoke of not wanting the child, Surya's son was born of her. The god vanished from Kunti's presence and returned to his chariot in the eastern sky.

The sound of gurgling laughter made Kunti look down at her feet. There she saw what seemed the most beautiful baby in the world! He laughed up at her. His skin gleamed golden brown in the sun and in his earlobes were dazzling gold earrings. Next to the baby lay a suit of golden armour.

The baby held up his arms to Kunti, but she turned away and wept. She was so unhappy about what people would say that she hardened her heart and decided to get rid of the baby. She had brought a basket of clothes to the river, so that she could get changed after her bathe. Now she emptied this basket and placed in it both the baby and the golden armour.

Kunti took one last look at the baby. "Forgive me, little one," she whispered. Then she pushed the basket into the water. As she watched it floating down the river she wept. Somehow she felt that she was no longer a child.

In time Kunti grew up to be a lovely young woman, and married Raja Pandu, the good king of Hastinapura. When Pandu knew that he could have no children of his own, she told him about the prayer that Durvasa had taught her. At Pandu's request she used the prayer to have sons by different gods. You can read about them in other stories in this book. All these sons turned out to be noble princes, so Kunti should have been happy. But she always remained grave as though some secret sorrow weighed on her heart. She longed of course, to know what had happened to her first child.

On that sad day, the basket containing the baby had floated down river with the current. A humble charioteer named Adhiratha who was walking by the river bank saw a basket bobbing up and down on the water. Curious, he waded into the river and pulled the basket to the shore. On peeping inside it, he was amazed to see a beautiful baby boy lying fast asleep. He rushed home with the basket.

"Look, Radha," the charioteer called to his wife, "look what I found on the river! The gods must have pitied our childless state and sent us this baby!"

"How perfect he is!" cried his excited wife.

They named the child Karna. Carefully they put away the golden armour so that he could wear it when he was older. They found that the glittering gold earrings could not be removed, they seemed to be part of his ears.

From childhood Karna was known for his skill with weapons. When he wore the Sun-god's golden armour, none could wound him in any fight. He grew up believing that his parents were Adhiratha and Radha. But Surya watched his human son from the sky and his life-giving rays bathed Karna every day in light and warmth. The boy grew stronger and stronger.

"Father, I want to be a great warrior," said Karna. "Who is the best teacher in the land?"

"Son, Drona is the best in the land. But he will never accept a poor charioteer's son as his student. He teaches the princes of Hastinapura archery, fencing, club wielding, wrestling and all the other skills a warrior needs."

Nevertheless, Karna approached Drona. "Sir, I am Karna, the son of Adhiratha the charioteer. I humbly beg to become your pupil."

But it was as Adhiratha had warned him. Proud Drona would not agree to take a pupil from such a poor home and Karna left disappointed. But Surya's son did not give up. He was determined to become a great warrior and some day challenge Drona's best and favourite pupil, Prince Arjuna, to single combat. Karna learned that Drona had studied the science of warfare from the mighty Parasurama. Parasurama was still alive, though an old hermit living now in the Mahendra Hills. The teacher must be at least as great as the pupil, Karna reasoned.

There was one problem. Parasurama accepted only the sons of teachers and priests as his pupils, for he was known to hate the children of soldiers, and charioteers counted as soldiers because they often drove their chariots into battle. Karna had told Drona the truth about his father and been rejected. "Parasurama will never accept me as a pupil either, if he knows who I am," thought the boy. This time Karna decided to tell a lie.

So Parasurama was led to believe that Karna was the son of a teacher, like himself, and he agreed to accept him as a pupil. While Parasurama found him an eager pupil and quick to learn, Karna also served his teacher with great devotion, working hard and anticipating his every wish. Pleased with such devotion, Parasurama taught him all he knew, including secret military strategies.

One day when they were far from home the old teacher became very tired and sleepy.

"Please lie down, Sir, on this grass," suggested Karna, "and rest your head on my lap."

Now, while Parasurama slept, a vicious insect came and began biting Karna on his thigh. Anxious not to disturb his teacher, Karna sat perfectly still, but the insect kept boring a deeper hole. At last, Karna's blood trickling from his thigh wet Parasurama's head and he woke up.

"Dear Karna, you are bleeding!" cried the old man. "Why did you not wake me earlier and kill the insect?"

Then, suddenly, Parasurama became suspicious. "Tell me, are you really a teacher's son?" he asked. "The pain must have been dreadful! Yet you sat like a statue and made no sound. No teacher's son could have endured such pain in the way that you did! Tell me who you really are."

Karna felt that he could no longer keep the truth from his teacher. Besides, he thought he had already got what he wanted from him. So he told Parasurama that his father was a charioteer called Adhiratha.

"Ah, Karna you have cheated me!" Parasurama cried. "Charioteers, however humble, are also soldiers. You must know that all who are children of soldiers are my sworn enemies. The only reason that I do not kill you now with my bare hands is because you have served me faithfully like a son!"

The teacher's anger was terrible. He placed on Karna a curse saying that, great warrior though he had now become, in his hour of most desperate need Karna would forget every military skill and strategy learnt from him. "You will die in battle, and be unable to save yourself by all you have learnt dishonestly. Now leave my presence!"

Karna replied that to die in battle was no curse, but a blessing for a warrior! He thanked Parasurama most respectfully for all he had learnt, and left him.

In Hastinapura, Drona decided to put on an exhibition when his pupils, the five Pandava princes and the hundred Kaurava princes, could display their skill with weapons. Everyone at the court was present, and a great crowd gathered to watch. All the displays were spectacular, but the performance of Prince Arjuna, who could use both left and right hand with equal ease, amazed and delighted the audience most. Duryodhana, the eldest Kaurava prince, seethed with hatred. While he himself was no match for Arjuna, he desperately wished that there was someone who could beat this cousin whose skills seemed superhuman. It did not help when Drona publicly boasted that there was none to match Arjuna in all the world.

Suddenly a voice from the crowd thundered, "I am a greater warrior!" The crowd made way for a tall and handsome youth who walked confidently up to the princes. Kunti, who had a place of honour in the audience, looked at the godlike Karna. His face seemed to shine. She saw the glittering earrings and the golden armour, and recognised the son she had abandoned so long ago. With a little cry she fainted and had to be carried into the palace.

But Karna was not distracted by this. One by one and with the greatest of ease, he performed every one of Arjuna's displays with all the different weapons. Drona was forced to admit, reluctantly, that this strange youth was at least the equal of his best pupil.

Duryodhana was overjoyed. He embraced the stranger and swore eternal friendship.

Karna turned to Arjuna and, not knowing that the Pandava prince was his own younger brother, he challenged him to single combat. "Come, let us fight and prove who is the better warrior."

Arjuna began to get ready for the fight, but Drona felt uneasy and stepped in.

"Stranger, you are indeed a mighty warrior and I salute you, but first tell us who you are. You look familiar and yet I cannot remember meeting you before this day. Prince Arjuna is the third son of Rani Kunti and Raja Pandu. He is very nobly born. What of yourself? The rules of single combat are that only those of equal birth may fight each other."

Karna realised that his humble birth again stood in his way. In his bitterness, he could not immediately reply.

Duryodhana noted Karna's silence and bowed head. For once in his life the Kaurava prince did a most noble thing - although his reason for helping Karna may have been selfish. He came forward and gripped Karna's hand.

"I have already sworn my undying friendship to you. Let me now share part of my kingdom with you and make you a king." He turned and addressed the crowd: "Respected elders, gentle lords and ladies, people of Hastinapura, know that this day I give this man all the land in Anga. My brave friend is the king of Anga and there is no man who is not his equal!"

Karna now spied his poor old father, Adhiratha, at the back of the crowd. He ran forward to greet him and bowed to him as a dutiful son should. Adhiratha embraced the shining warrior.

Karna raised his head and spoke with pride to Drona

and the princes: "I am not ashamed of my birth. I am Karna the son of Adhiratha. My father is a fine charioteer and a good man."

Drona remembered the proud boy whom he had refused to teach some years ago. "King of Anga you may now be," he said to Karna, "but your birth is not royal. You may not fight Arjuna in single combat."

To Karna's great disappointment the exhibition was declared over, and the crowd dispersed.

"I can never repay your generosity," said Karna to Duryodhana, "but as long as there is strength in my arm, it will be at your service. From now on your enemies will be my enemies, your cause will be my cause." Duryodhana could not have been more delighted. With the help of this mighty hero, he hoped, in time, to defeat his cousins the Pandava princes.

As king of Anga, Karna now gave his parents a palace to live in and provided all the comforts that they could wish.

Indra, king of the gods, grew more and more worried for Arjuna, who was his son by Rani Kunti. "As long as he is alive, Karna is a threat to my son," he thought and plotted ways to reduce his power.

One morning, just as Karna was sitting down to pray, as was his daily custom, a beggar came to his door. The previous night Surya, the Sun, had appeared to Karna in a dream and warned him on no account to give anything to a beggar that day. But Karna who was the soul of generosity, could not refuse to help a beggar, and asked him what he wanted.

"King of Anga, you are famous for your kindness, but I have a very great favour to ask of you," whined the beggar, who was none other than Indra in disguise.

"Do not fear," said Karna, "whatever you want I shall give you, if it is mine to give."

Indra knew that the Sun-god had given Karna his special armour and earrings to protect him in battle. As long as Karna wore them, no one could kill or wound him. The beggar now asked Karna for the armour and earrings.

"They can be of no use to you," said Karna, "whereas they are very valuable to me. Are you sure that you want them? If you want gold, I can give you plenty of it, but my earrings are part of my ears and cannot be removed."

The beggar insisted that he wanted the armour and the earrings. So Karna gave him the magic armour and then without hesitation cut off his earlobes and presented the earrings to the beggar who stood with outstretched arms.

Indra felt quite ashamed of himself as he saw such noble behaviour. He revealed his real self and Karna fell to his knees in worship.

"Mighty Karna," said Indra, "you have truly a kingly nature. Your generosity must put other princes to shame. Today you have even made a beggar of the king of heaven!"

In spite of himself, Indra felt that he should give the good king something in return for his golden armour and earrings. So he offered him one wish.

Karna asked for Indra's supreme weapon, the spear, Shakti, with which he killed all enemies. Indra was not so generous as Karna. He agreed only to loan it to Karna. "You may use this weapon once only against any enemy you choose. But the moment it is used, it will return to me in heaven." With this gift Indra vanished.

In course of time the enmity between the Kauravas and the Pandavas increased to such a level that war broke out between the cousins. True to his promise of friendship with Duryodhana, Karna sided with the Kauravas. The great battle of Kurukshetra was fought.

To the dismay of the Kauravas the Pandava army included a band of demons led by Ghatotkacha, Bhima's demon-son.

"Karna, this demon is terrifying our soldiers. If only you can kill him, the rest of the demon troop will be without a leader and will return to the forest from which they came. This is not their war. They are only here because of Ghatotkacha whose demon-mother married Bhima in the forest," said Duryodhana.

So Karna turned his attention to Ghatotkacha, the young giant whose appearance and bloodcurdling cries so chilled and frightened the Kauravas. Bravely Surya's son rushed at Ghatotkacha, only to be flung some distance by the giant. Without his magic armour and earrings, he was wounded in battle for the first time in his life. Now Ghatotkacha advanced on him with a huge club raised in one hand. Karna grabbed the first weapon to hand and hurled it at Ghatotkacha. The spear he threw was Indra's weapon, Shakti. Karna had been meaning to keep the spear for use against his rival Arjuna, but now it killed Bhima's son instead and then vanished from sight. Shakti had returned to its owner, Indra the king of heaven.

In the fierce fighting, Drona, the Kaurava general, was killed. Duryodhana then asked Karna, his friend the king of Anga, to take command of the Kaurava army. Karna agreed.

At the beginning of the war Kunti had blessed all the Pandava princes: "Go my sons and fight for justice. God will surely give you victory!" But her heart was heavy. If the Pandavas won, then Karna their eldest brother would have to lose! How many of her fine sons, she wondered, would survive this terrible war? Having sent her first baby floating down the river, Kunti had lavished a special love and tenderness on her other sons. The world believed her to be a model mother, as she had been a model wife. Kunti secretly shuddered to think of her sons now in opposite camps. They might even kill each other in battle! She could not bear the thought.

When Kunti heard that Karna had been made the Kaurava general and had sworn to engage Arjuna in combat during the battle the following day, she felt that her heart must break. If Arjuna and Karna, the two greatest heroes of the armies, fought each other, one of them must surely die! Kunti knew that she had to do something about it.

She dressed herself in a cheap dark sari so that she looked like a poor serving woman. As night fell she pulled the sari low over her head so that her face was hidden and silently made her way to the Kaurava camp. There were so many tents! Kunti despaired of finding the right one. If she was caught by an enemy soldier - what explanation could she give for wandering about in their camp at night! She dared not enter any tent but Karna's.

But Kunti was in luck. As the moon came from behind a cloud she saw Karna's flag fluttering over a tent. Only Karna had a flag with a blazing sun painted on it. Surya's son had always honoured and worshipped the sun, without knowing that the Sun-god was his father.

Kunti entered the tent. Karna was a light sleeper and, on hearing a slight rustle, immediately sprang to his feet. He saw a woman standing inside his tent.

"Who are you and why have you come like a thief in the night? Are you some spy sent by the Pandavas? Did you think to kill me while I slept?"

Kunti could not speak or move for a little while. She was too overcome with emotion at being with her lost son after so many years.

"Who are you?" repeated Karna. "Why do you hide your treacherous face?" With a swift movement of his hand, he lifted away the sari-cloth covering her face. Rani Kunti stared back at him.

"Forgive me, queen," said Karna, kneeling, "for any disrespect that I may have shown you. I am only a rough soldier and do not have the fine manners of your son, Yudhishtira. But then, he was born to be a king, while I was born a charioteer's son."

"You are every bit as noble as any of my sons," came Kunti's soft reply.

Karna rose and walked away from the queen.

"Lady, you honour me," said Karna, "but you have come to my tent at night, when we have never even met, no doubt for some very important reason. Why should Yudhishtira's mother make this dangerous journey?"

"I have seen you before," said Kunti, not answering his question.

"When? Where?" said Karna.

"I saw you in your golden armour years ago at the exhibition that Drona held," said Kunti, remembering much more than that day.

"Then you must know that the world laughed at me that day," said Karna, bitterly. "I challenged your son, the high-born Prince Arjuna, to single combat! But I was not his equal, they said, because my father was a charioteer."

"Oh, Karna! Forget your bitterness!" cried Kunti. "Nothing would please me more than to see you friendly with the Pandavas. Please come away and join forces with my sons."

"It is too late for friendship with your sons," said Karna. "They are fighting the Kauravas who are my friends."

"But this battle for the throne of Hastinapura concerns only the Pandavas and the Kauravas. Even should the Kauravas win, how can it benefit you? I feel like a mother to you, Karna. That is why I have come to advise you to do the right thing. Give up the Kauravas and join my sons, for justice is on the Pandava side. The throne belongs to Yudhishtira, and the Kauravas are cheating him of what is his." Kunti spoke as persuasively as she could.

"How very much you honour me, Yudhishtira's mother, to think of me as your son!" spoke Karna, smiling, but his eyes were hard and glittering. "Then let me tell you with complete frankness, as a son would to his mother, I already know that your sons are in the right and the Kauravas are in the wrong, in this case. But you cannot persuade me to change sides in this war. Even Krishna came to argue with me in the beginning. Justice is on the side of the Pandavas and that is why he is in the battle, driving Arjuna's war chariot and helping the Pandavas against the Kauravas who are equally his cousins. But I give you the answer that I gave to the wise king of Dwarka. I have found that this world is not a very just place. I do not fight for justice. I fight for honour and friendship. I owe Duryodhana more than life itself. He has been like a brother to me. So even though I know that he is wrong, I will still support him. But do not fear, Yudhishtira's mother! God will give the Pandavas victory in the end and your son will surely become a king."

Kunti felt herself at a loss for words. At length she asked him, "Karna, why do you keep calling me 'Yudhishtira's mother'?"

"Why, have I failed in courtesy, lady?" replied Karna, with exaggerated politeness. "Is it not the custom to address a woman as the mother of her eldest son? And are you not pleased to hear the name of Yudhishtira on men's lips? All mothers love their first-born with the deepest love and I am sure that an excellent prince like Yudhishtira well merits your love."

"Oh stop, stop!" cried Kunti, covering her ears. "Cruel Karna, Yudhishtira is not my eldest son!" No longer able to keep the truth from Karna she told him of his birth, and continued, "So the Pandavas are your younger brothers! Now that you know the truth you must see that you cannot possibly fight them," said the queen. "But forgive me, my son, for the terrible wrong that I did you. Understand why I did it and pity me."

Karna too had a confession to make: "Forgive me, lady, for causing you any pain tonight. I already knew the secret of my birth, but I waited to see if you would admit it to me. Some days ago I saluted Lord Surya as he rose in the eastern sky. To my wonder and joy the Sun-god appeared to me in person. He told me how I was born and later adopted. He came to warn me that the Kauravas are doomed to fail in this war. Like you and Krishna, he also asked me to make my peace with Yudhishtira and join the Pandava side." Karna did not add that his father the Sun had also commanded him to be gentle and gracious to his mother, should he ever come across her, but he remembered this now.

"My answer is still 'no', royal lady," said Surya's son. "After all these years, you tell me of brothers and call me 'son'. How can my feelings change all at once? I am still the child of Radha and Adhiratha. Duryodhana has been like a brother. I can never betray him."

Kunti wept to hear his words. She had tried so hard, but Karna seemed so strong and unbending.

"I see that nothing I can say will move you. I do not blame you for not listening to me, Karna. I never gave you a mother's love, so why should I expect it of you now? But I beg you to think of your innocent brothers - how have they harmed you? Knowing they are your brothers, how can you kill them?"

Karna looked into the tear-filled eyes of the queen and was moved by her appeal. The words of the Sun-god rang in his ears. "Be gentle and gracious to your mother, for she has suffered much."

"I have given my word and must fight Arjuna tomorrow," he told her, "but I also promise you that I shall not harm any of my brothers. And now I must rest a little for it will soon be morning and I shall lead the Kaurava army into battle. Come, mother," said Kunti's first-born son at last, "I will escort you to the Pandava camp."

Karna fought with great bravery the following day. But he was killed by an arrow shot by Arjuna who did not know of their relationship. From then on the Kauravas began to lose.

When the Pandavas at last won the war, they honoured all their dead, including Ghatotkacha - Bhima's son - and Abhimanyu - Arjuna's son. Rani Kunti then told them about her secret son.

"Honour Karna, your eldest brother," she said. "He was the most generous of men!"

For Love of Urvashi

R AJA Pururavas was king of Kurukshetra a long, long, time ago. Not only was he a very handsome man, he had many good qualities too. He was a loyal friend, a gracious host and a just and merciful ruler. Loving all things beautiful, he encouraged artists, sculptors, musicians and gardeners to produce many fine works of art. It was his pleasure to make his little kingdom as much like heaven on earth as was possible. Above all, the king was noted for his patience and determination.

Pururavas especially loved the peace and natural beauty of the forests, so whenever his duties as a king allowed, he would slip away quietly for a ride in the nearby forest. When wandering there one morning, his ears caught the faint sound of musical laughter. Then he heard it again. Feeling very curious, Pururavas dismounted, tied his horse to a tree and walked very softly in the direction of the enchanting sound.

He came upon a scene such as one only views in dreams. There before his astonished eyes was a clearing in the forest which looked like a jewelled park, and here some beautiful maidens were playing, throwing a golden ball to each other.

"Surely such beauty is not of this world!" Pururavas thought. "Perhaps I have died and entered heaven?" and he pinched himself to make sure he was awake.

He hid behind some bushes and observed the maidens more closely. They looked so happy and carefree, laughing frequently and moving with such lightness and grace!

They had large beautiful eyes and their lovely dark hair floated down in waves to their slim waists. Their shining saris seemed to be made of sheerest gossamer. Their voices were the sweetest the king had ever heard. The beauty of the lady nearest him quite took away his breath! "She must be a goddess!" thought Pururavas.

Unable to stop himself, he stepped out from behind the bush where he was hiding. The slight rustling of leaves distracted the maiden and she failed to catch the golden ball which fell and rolled to Pururavas's feet.

"Oh!" exclaimed the maiden in surprise, as Pururavas handed her the ball. "Who are you?"

"Urvashi, he must be a *gandharva*," called one of the others, convinced that so handsome a man could only be a heavenly being like themselves. "Ask him to join us."

But Urvashi gazed at the stranger in stunned silence. Time stood still for both Pururavas and Urvashi as they looked deep into each other's eyes.

"O sisters, he is no *gandharva*!" cried another maiden in alarm. "He is a man. Come, let us fly away!" The maidens seemed to rise in the air.

"Urvashi, dear sister, come away with us," they pleaded.

But Urvashi and the young king had lost their hearts to each other.

"Stay with me, goddess," begged the king. "All my life I have searched for someone like you. You have brought spring to the forest and sunshine to my heart."

Urvashi blushed and laughed. "I am no goddess," she explained. My name is Urvashi. My sisters and I are *apsaras*. We sing and dance at Lord Indra's court. We thought at first that you were one of the *gandharvas*. They are our brothers and are the musicians of heaven."

The *apsaras* sighed to see Urvashi looking lovesick and talking so foolishly with a mere man. "Goodbye, sister," they called and flew up into the vast blue sky, sure that she would soon recover her senses and join them.

For the rest of the day Pururavas used all his charm to woo the *apsara*. "I may only be a man, but I will love you as long as I live. I cannot give you heaven, but, if you marry me, you shall have all that love can provide."

Urvashi's mind told her that marriage between a man and an *apsara* was doomed to fail. "Will you give up the comforts of Indra's glittering heaven to live on earth? Won't you miss the *apsaras*, the *gandharvas*, and the gods and goddesses who are your constant companions? Will you give up the sweet ambrosia of heaven for earthly food and drink?" she asked herself. But her heart would not listen. "Give happiness a chance!" it cried.

"Gentle king," she said at last, a sad catch in her voice, "it is impossible for a man and an *apsara* always to be together. You are young now, but you will age and some day die, while I will remain forever just as I am today."

"One lifetime with you will be happiness enough for me," replied Pururavas, "if you can bear the pain of separation when I die."

"Alas, we may not have even one full lifetime together," said Urvashi. "I may only live with you on one condition. If you break it, then I must fly back to heaven."

Pururavas learnt that the condition was that Urvashi must never see him naked. If she did, she would have to leave him. This seemed simple enough to him! Surely he could keep it without difficulty.

By nightfall Urvashi had agreed to marry the king, and they were soon married amid great pomp and splendour, and general rejoicing by the people.

For some years they knew great happiness and their marriage was blessed with children. Then Pururavas began to lose interest in his kingly duties and to leave more and more tasks to his ministers. It was almost as if he knew that he might lose Urvashi soon and felt a desperate need to spend every moment with her.

In the rare moments, too, that Urvashi was not with her husband, sad thoughts would crowd into her mind. "My lord is now in the prime of life, but daily he grows older and draws nearer to Yama, stern god of Death," thought the beautiful queen. "Can I bear to watch him age and then die?" Also she keenly missed the other *apsaras* and *gandharvas*. In the king's presence she hid her sorrows well, determined to do all she could to make him as happy as she possibly could. Their palace was bright and colourful. Urvashi danced and sang enchanting songs to please the king. The strength of her love drew him like a magnet. No wonder that Pururavas was always by her side!

The *apsaras* and the *gandharvas* had not forgotten their sister either. They had had to cut themselves off when she married a man, but they were convinced that she would soon tire of her human husband and return to them. They were surprised when this did not happen and they missed her sorely. Heaven was not the same without Urvashi! At length Indra asked the *gandharvas* to bring the beautiful dancer back to his court.

The *apsaras* advised, "It is useless to reason with her. Urvashi's love has trapped her on earth. If you kill Raja Pururavas in order to release her, she may never forgive you."

"Then think of some other solution," Indra suggested.

The *gandharvas* hatched a mischievous plot. Knowing the condition which would cause Urvashi to leave her husband, they decided that she must see Pururavas naked.

Now Urvashi kept in the palace a pair of young lambs as pets. At night they lay on silken cushions in a corner of the bedroom where she and Pururavas slept. One night the *gandharvas* stole into the palace and crept into the royal bedchamber. They picked up the lambs, as if to steal them, and their frightened bleating awoke the king and queen.

"My sweet pets are being stolen!" exclaimed the queen.

"Do not fear, beloved," assured Pururavas. "I'll catch the thieves."

The angry king pushed aside the coverings, jumped out of bed, without stopping to put on any clothes, and gave immediate chase. This was the moment that the *gandharva* thieves had hoped for. With Indra's help, a flash of lightning lit up the room. Pururavas froze in his tracks and looked back at his wife for one long moment of horror.

The room plunged back into darkness. A sweet and sorrowful voice said, "Farewell, my husband."

"No!" shouted the king, but silence was the only reply.

Pururavas's pain was terrible. He was like a madman. He turned his palace inside out searching for Urvashi. He looked for her in the forests, too. His family and ministers despaired to see him so crazed with grief.

His chief minister tried to recall him to normal life. "Your Majesty, you must not forget that you are a king! You have a duty to your people! We need you. There are other beautiful women that you can marry."

At length Pururavas replied, "You do well to remind me of my duties, friend. Why should Kurukshetra suffer for my loss? My people deserve a better king than I can be. My son shall be that king and profit by your wise counsel."

So a very young prince came to the throne of Kurukshetra and Pururavas roamed the forests like a vagabond, calling out over and over again the beloved name of Urvashi. He realised that she must be back in her own timeless world of the *apsaras* and *gandharvas*, but he hoped that some day she might visit the earth again, and wherever he went he asked the trees, the birds and other animals, if they had seen his Urvashi.

In time Pururavas's wanderings brought him to Lake Anyatahplaksha. The sight of the cool blue water with graceful swans gliding on it calmed him. It was evening and he was weary from his travels. He decided that the bank of the lake would be a good place to rest.

Just as he was falling asleep, Pururavas heard some voices amid the splashing of water. He pretended to turn in his sleep, but from the corner of his eye he spied a miracle. One by one the swans swam ashore and changed into beautiful *apsaras*! Urvashi, his wife, was among them. With great difficulty Pururavas lay perfectly still.

"Urvashi, isn't this the man who stole your heart?" whispered an *apsara*.

The voice he remembered so well, answered, "Yes, indeed, this is my husband, the noble Raja Pururavas. He has given away his kingdom for love of me and now he wanders from place to place searching for me. How exhausted he is! Poor man! See how his feet are bleeding from thorns! Sisters, I must bathe his feet."

"No, Urvashi, he will wake if you do. You know that we must be gone before he wakes."

But Urvashi pleaded with the *apsaras* to fly away and leave her with Pururavas. "This is the last night of the year. For just this one night let me enjoy love and happiness. If you keep my secret, no one will miss me till the morning, and I will be back before then."

"Urvashi, you have lost your place on earth," warned

an *apsara*. "Beware that you do not now lose your place in heaven!"

In the end the gentle and kind *apsaras* promised to keep her secret, and they flew away.

In great joy Pururavas embraced his wife and they spent a happy night together. Towards dawn Urvashi gave her husband some instructions and flew away.

Pururavas bathed and prayed - and waited. Later that day, as Urvashi had told him, he saw a group of shining *gandharvas* descend from the sky. He received them very politely.

The leader of the group addressed him: "Hail, Raja Pururavas! Your courtesy puts us to shame. Know that we are the ones who came as thieves in the night to steal your queen's pet lambs. We can no longer live with this on our consciences. Yesterday while you slept, some *apsaras* saw you. It was their suggestion that we see you and confess our wicked deed. Our only excuse is one that you may understand - we love Urvashi, too, and wanted her back in heaven. So we tricked you. But now we know the hurt we have caused you both, and beg forgiveness. We cannot undo the past, but we can grant you one wish in compensation. Ask us for anything: long life, riches, forgetfulness - anything to make your life more bearable."

Pururavas asked to become a *gandharva*. Nothing else would do. Urvashi had advised him to make this wish.

"Very well," agreed the *gandharvas*.

The heavenly musicians now helped Pururavas to perform some difficult sacrifices and recite some secret charms. At last he too became a *gandharva* and flew up to Indra's heaven with his new companions. Urvashi was waiting to welcome him to Heaven, where they live together in love and joy forever.